I Gave My Heart To A Jersey Killa 3

Tina J

Copyright 2019

This novel is a work of fiction. Any resemblances to actual events, real people, living or dead, organizations, establishments or locales are products of the author's imagination. Other names, characters, places, and incidents are used fictionally.

All parts reserved. No part of this book may be used or reproduced in any form or by any means electronic or mechanical, including photocopying, recording or by information storage and retrieval system, without written permission from the publisher and write.

Because of the dynamic nature of the Internet, any web address or links contained in this book may have changed since publication, and may no longer be valid.

Warning:

This book is strictly Urban Fiction and the story is **NOT**

REAL!

Characters will not behave the way you want them to; nor will they react to situations the way you think they should. Some of them may be drug addicts, kingpins, savages, thugs, rich, poor, ho's, sluts, haters, bitter ex-girlfriends or boyfriends, people from the past and the list can go on and on. That is what Urban Fiction mostly consists of. If this isn't anything you foresee yourself interested in, then do yourself a favor and don't read it because it's only going to piss you off. □□

Also, the book will not end the way you want so please be advised that the outcome will be based solely on my own thoughts and ideas. I hope you enjoy this book that y'all made me write. Thanks so much to my readers, supporters, publisher and fellow authors and authoress for the support. □□

Author Tina J

More books from me:

The Thug I Chose 1, 2 & 3

A Thin Line Between Me and My Thug 1 & 2

I Got Luv For My Shawty 1 & 2

Kharis and Caleb: A Different Kind of Love 1 & 2

Loving You Is A Battle 1 & 2 & 3

Violet and The Connect 1 & 2 & 3

You Complete Me

Love Will Lead You Back

This Thing Called Love

Are We In This Together 1,2 &3

Shawty Down To Ride For a Boss 1, 2 &3

When A Boss Falls in Love 1, 2 & 3

Let Me Be The One 1 & 2

We Got That Forever Love

Aint No Savage Like The One I Got 1&2

A Queen and A Hustla 1, 2 & 3

Thirsty For A Bad Boy 1&2

Hassan and Serena: An Unforgettable Love 1&2

Caught Up Loving A Beast 1, 2 & 3

A Street King And His Shawty 1 & 2

I Fell For The Wrong Bad Boy 1&2

I Wanna Love You 1 & 2

Addicted to Loving a Boss 1, 2, & 3

I Need That Gangsta Love 1&2

Creepin With The Plug 1 & 2

All Eyes On The Crown 1,2&3

When She's Bad, I'm Badder: Jiao and Dreek, A Crazy

Love Story 1,2&3

Still Luvin A Beast 1&2

Her Man, His Savage 1 & 2

Marco & Rakia: Not Your Ordinary, Hood Kinda Love 1,2

& 3

Feenin For A Real One 1, 2 & 3

A Kingpin's Dynasty 1, 2 & 3

What Kinda Love Is This: Captivating A Boss 1, 2 & 3

Frankie & Lexi: Luvin A Young Beast 1, 2 & 3

A Dope Boys Seduction 1, 2 & 3

My Brother's Keeper 1. 2 & 3

C'Yani & Meek: A Dangerous Hood Love 1, 2 & 3

When A Savage Falls for A Good Girl 1, 2 & 3

Eva & Deray 1 & 2

Blame It On His Gangsta Luv 1 & 2

Falling For The Wrong Hustla 1, 2 & 3

I Gave My Heart To A Jersey Killa 1, 2 & 3

Previously…

VJ

I paced the hospital floor a million times waiting on them to tell me if my son and girl were ok. When Monie hit the wall and passed out, all I saw was her ex abusing her again.

I jumped on her cousin and didn't give a fuck who got in it. I was over the childish shit he said and did. It's obvious he was testing me and even with my arm losing feeling every now and then, it didn't stop me from getting his ass.

The gun went off and I immediately ran over to her and my son. Legend was crying and he seemed to be ok but Monie was still knocked out, which broke my heart. She's been through so much and her own cousin accidentally hit her.

Even I know it wasn't on purpose, but he had no business swinging off anyway. Then, if my son weren't strapped in, he would've fallen out the seat and that had me hot.

I don't know who told them what happened but my parents, Ariel's and some of my cousins were pulling in at the same time we did. They all loved Armonie and stalked me for Legend to come over.

"Mr. Davis." The pediatrician came in to give me the results of the tests.

"Yes." She smiled and put her index finger in between my sons' hand.

"Legend here is going to be fine. He has a tiny scratch on his forehead which can possibly be from the tag on the seat or he may have done it. All the tests were normal and he's ok to go home." My mom stood and rubbed my back.

"Thanks. Is his mom ok?"

"Go check on her VJ. I'll stay with Legend and we'll be over when she gives me his discharge papers." My mom said.

"A'ight and pops don't hold him the whole time." He told me to leave. Him and Armonie were spoiling the shit outta my son. I thought it would be my mom, but my father can't seem to get enough. I mean he comes over everyday if we don't bring him by.

I told the doctor my mother could sign the paper work and thanked her for taking care of my son. I went into the regular emergency department and requested for them to buzz me in the back.

At first, they asked my name. I didn't know why until the receptionist said her mom has a name written down of a person who she didn't want to visit her. I had no doubt it was Haven.

"Where is she?" I asked her father who was sitting there with her siblings.

"My mom took her to the bathroom." Her sister told me.

"Is she ok? What are they saying?"

"She has a slight concussion and a busted lip." My fist balled up as her dad continued telling me what the doctor said. I leaned against the wall.

"Nobody blames you VJ. You had enough and did what you had to for your family." Her pops said.

"We good bro." Colby Jr said and gave me a man hug with his other brother. Her younger sister smiled and said I need to give Monie more kids because everybody being stingy with Legend.

"VJ?" Monie ran to me and I picked her up.

"You ok? You need anything?" She shook her head no and cried on my neck. Her family stepped out.

"Legend is with my parents. They're discharging him soon."

"Is be ok? Did he fall out the seat?" I closed the door and laid her in the bed.

"No. He has a scratch on his forehead. She said he may have done it himself; otherwise he's fine. Let me see." I moved the hair out her face and got mad all over again seeing her lip and the knot on her forehead.

"I'm ok babe. What about you?" She said her mom mentioned me and Haven fighting.

"Never worry about me. I'm good as long as you and my son good."

"I'm always gonna worry about my fiancé." She smiled and I couldn't help but do the same.

Last night after making love to her, I proposed. Yup, she had my son six weeks ago and I damn sure nut all in her so we could have another one.

She was lying on her side in front of me when I decided to pop the question.

"Monie, what you doing for the rest of your life?" She turned around and her mouth fell open. She lifted herself on her elbows and then sat all the way up. I opened the box and showed her the 10-carat princess cut, yellow diamond I purchased her two weeks ago. I got her the Tesla as a push gift, but I had yet to give her a gift of my own.

"It's been a long and crazy year, but I'd do it all over again if you're the woman it's with. In this short time, you had me fall in love with you, delivered my son and made me the happiest man alive. Would you do me the honors of being my wife?" She nodded and allowed the tears to fall.

"I won't mess up baby." I told her and put the ring on.

"I want to tell them at dinner tomorrow. Is that ok?" She asked staring at the ring.

"Anything you wanna do, I'm down." I kissed her and the two of us fell asleep holding each other.

She was supposed to mention it tonight but decided to wait when Ariel announced her pregnancy. She didn't wanna ruin the moment.

As of right now, my family are the only ones who knew and that's because my mom and aunt helped me pick the ring. I couldn't tell Ariel because she would've told.

"Do you still wanna marry me?" She looked up and wiped her tears.

"Monie that man don't dictate our relationship. Shit, if you wanted to get married right now, I'd go get the reverend guy who works here and do it. I love you Monie."

"I'm so sorry you're dealing with my cousin. I don't know what's wrong with him." I put both of my hands on her face.

"You can't worry about him; I'm not." She nodded and wrapped her arms around my neck.

"Here." I took the ring out my pocket and placed it back on her finger. She had it in the baby bag at her parents' house but again, she never got the chance to mention it.

"You got something to tell me?" Her father came through the door.

"I said yes." She smiled real big and flashed her ring.

"Oh my God. Sweetie you're getting married?" Her mom and sister ran over.

"You did good son in law." He and I had a discussion before I brought the ring. He voiced his concerns and I answered everyone truthfully. He gave me his blessing and now his daughter is about to be my wife.

"Treat her right." Colby Jr said and hugged her.

"Where's Legend?" Monie asked and we looked at the door. Ariel was walking him in.

"I'm sorry Armonie. I didn't know he was gonna act up." She started tearing up and handed my son to Colby Jr.

"What's wrong?"

"He told me to get rid of the baby because I said we were over." I felt Monie squeeze my hand and look at me. She mouthed the words *please don't leave*. Brayden had an aggravated look on his face as well. Haven is his best friend,

I'm his cousin and Ariel's his sister. I'm sure it's a lot for him to deal with.

"Ok Ms. Banks. I'm going to discharge you." The doctor scooted his way through everyone and gave her the aftercare instructions. They all stepped out while she got dressed.

"I'm gonna talk to him." I knew she meant her cousin.

"Not right now you're not." Her eyes met mine.

"He needs to cool off and accident or not, he needs to apologize to you Monie." She nodded.

"I'm serious. Not only did he hit you but he's making it uncomfortable for you when I'm there." I could care less but she didn't like the tension.

"You're right. Do you feel like taking a bath with me at home?" I knew it relaxed her.

"After I put Legend to bed, I'll do whatever you want." I smirked when she removed the gown and her breasts were bare. I loved sucking on her tities.

"Don't play Monie. You know I'll fuck you right here." She was massaging her own breasts and making soft moans. I

14

lifted her on the table and was about to give her what she wanted. We heard the door open and stopped.

"You done?" Ariel asked.

"Yea. VJ helping me with my bra." After she put her shirt on, I opened the curtain and we stepped out. Once we got outside, it's like both of our families were there and we were having a party. The good thing is no one held a grudge toward the other over Haven.

"You ok honey?" Her aunt Passion ran over to her.

"I'm fine. Where's uncle Wolf?" She looked around.

"Him and your uncle Jax went to find Haven. When you left, he said some mean things to Ariel too." She looked at me.

"Don't even think about apologizing for him."

"I don't know why he's so angry."

"It's not for any of us to know but I don't blame you or anyone else and I don't want you blaming yourself."

"I'm trying not to but he's my son and..." She cried.

"Get your dramatic ass over here. The whole world knows Haven crazy so don't try and figure him out." Another woman said.

"Who's that?" I asked Monie. When I say it was a lot of people out here, it really was.

"My aunt Darlene. She's off the hook. Come on." I tried to carry her, but she said she's fine. Everyone ended up at my house drinking and having a good time. It made my fiancé smile and it's all I ever want for her. When they left, we put Legend to bed and took a bath like she requested.

****

"What the fuck you mean someone broke into the office?" I lifted Monie off my chest and sat up. We had Legend lying with us and I didn't wanna scare him.

"Mr. Davis, we're not sure how they got in but the office is destroyed and they took everything out the safe." Ashley said. She's the woman we left in charge down in VA. She came highly recommended and up until this very moment, we had no issues.

"How did they get in the safe? No one has the combination but me and my sister?" I picked my cell up and sent a message to Vanity.

"You're not going to believe this but per the security footage, they used some explosive device.

"You gotta be kidding me."

"I'm sending you the video now. The cops are still here as well. Is there anything you want me to tell them?"

"I'll be there shortly." I hung up and answered my cell for Vanity. After I told her what happened she volunteered to ride with me but I cut it short. I hung up with her and called my cousin.

"Yo!" The background was pretty loud.

"Where you at?" It was eight o clock on a Sunday morning, and he sounded as if he were at a club.

"Wifey wanted breakfast. You know these people talk loud as hell at restaurants. What's up?"

"I told him what happened as I got dressed. He asked if I wanted him to ride and I told him no. Mycah already text back saying he was waiting for me.

"I need you to check on Monie for me, if I'm not back tomorrow."

"You already know." I hung up, packed a few things and went downstairs where Monie was.

"I'm coming." She was packing a bag for Legend.

"Monie you need to stay home with our son." I appreciated how she had my back.

"What if the bitch sent someone there to do it and they're waiting for you. VJ you don't need to go alone." I stopped her from packing my son bag.

"I'll be back tomorrow or Tuesday."

"VJ something's not right. I mean all these years and you never had a break in. What if it's a set up?" I couldn't deny feeling the same way but until it's confirmed I couldn't say it's true.

"I'm gonna be fine. I'll even talk to you the whole way there." She was tapping her foot.

"Please let me go with you." She begged.

"Stop worrying Monie." I kissed her and fought with her about going, all the way to my car. She wasn't giving up.

18

"Go inside. I'm calling you." I showed her the phone dialing the house number.

"Please be careful." I kissed her and watched as she took her time walking to the door. We spoke the whole ride and once I got there, I had to hang up and call Mycah. He didn't answer so I sent him a text and went inside. The cops were gone but Ashley's car was still there. I walked in and Ashley had tears running down her face.

CLICK!

"Took you long enough to get here." My hands went up and when I turned around to see who it was, shocked wasn't the word.

Ariel

"What?" I opened the door for Haven. Neither of us called or sent a text message to the other all week.

"Move." He walked past me and sat on the couch.

"Is my cousin ok?" I folded my arms and stayed quiet.

"Ariel I'm not in the fucking mood. Is my cousin ok?" He barked.

"I shouldn't tell you shit but she's fine. You gave her a concussion and since she hit her face on the wall, her lip busted." He put his head back on the couch.

"You mean to tell me no one told you this entire time how she was?"

"My phones been off and I haven't been at work."

"What's going on with you Haven? Are you tryna make your family hate you?" He opened his eyes and looked at me.

"I don't care for him since that night in the restaurant."

"Haven it was your fault. Look." I plopped down on the seat across from him.

"VJ loves your cousin. I mean really loves her and she's not gonna invite you to her wedding if you don't stop this shit."

"Wedding?" He questioned.

"He asked her to marry him the night before the dinner and she accepted. Her intention was to tell everyone but you bullied me into taking a test and she didn't wanna spoil the moment." I went over to where he sat and lifted his face.

"She's never going to forgive you if you don't make it right with VJ." He didn't say anything.

"He's about to be her husband so if your plan was to scare him off because we all know per you and the guys in the family; no one is good enough for the women in your family but, he's not going anywhere." He chuckled.

"Mr. Banks gave his blessing. Haven its time you did too." I kissed his forehead and walked in the kitchen to get my food. I made a small meatloaf with mashed potatoes and string beans.

"Do I have to be his friend?" I jumped because he scared me.

"No. You never have to speak but talking shit and fighting him isn't the way to go. As you can see Monie will stay away and it's not fair to the family." I put some food on my plate and sat down to eat.

"Where's mine?" I blew on my food and ignored him.

"Ariel?"

"Haven, I didn't know you were coming and I'm still not speaking to you." I rolled my eyes.

"How you not speaking to me and we just had a whole conversation?" He went and got a fork out the drawer and started eating off my plate.

"You know what I'm talking about? How could you tell me to abort our baby?" I slammed the fork on the table and waited for him to answer.

"If you weren't gonna be with me, I wasn't about to let another nigga be around my kid." I shook my head because he's really crazy.

"Did you do it?" I ignored him.

"DID YOU?" He pounded on the table scaring me.

"No and stop doing that."

"Doing what?"

"Making me fear you. I don't like that." I never wanted to be in fear of a man I'm with. Monie went through it with Freddy and my aunt Maylan did with her ex too.

"My bad. Come here."

"No thanks." He gave me a look and instead of arguing, I stood in front of him. He lifted my shirt and rubbed my belly.

"How far are you?" He kissed it.

"Seven weeks."

"I felt the difference over a month ago so that's about right." I mushed him in the head and passed him the ultrasound photo.

"It looks like a pea." He was turning it upside down.

"You need to speak with Armonie." I started eating.

"I know. You coming?"

"Haven I'm not dressed and what you need me for?"

I sent a text to Armonie letting her know we were on our way because I'm not about to let him surprise her. She may not wanna see him right now and I hope VJ not there. If he is, she'll request to see him elsewhere.

She didn't respond so I finished eating. Afterwards, I went to see where Haven was, and he was passed out in the bed. I mean snoring and all. I sent a message back to Armonie and said, never mind we can do it another time because he fell asleep. I ended up getting in bed with him.

I don't forgive him just yet but I'm not gonna lie and say I don't miss laying under him.

****

RING! RING! I moved outta Haven's embrace to answer my phone. I don't know why I kept the old-fashioned ringtone. It's loud as hell.

"Hello."

"Hey Ariel. Carmen called out for the 7-7 shift for tomorrow. Do you mind covering?" My boss asked.

"Ok. I'll be there but I'm taking off for the next two days because it's my day off." I told her after looking at the clock.

"Ok. Thanks, and good night." I hung up, set the alarm for 5 am and went back to bed.

The next day, the alarm went off and it felt like I only slept an hour. I swear this baby had me tired all the time and these early morning shifts were killing me.

I got dressed, left Haven a note and headed to work. I text my boss this morning and she said I was working in the emergency room. It's where Carmen was scheduled. I couldn't wait for my dad's building to be done, and I could make my own hours.

I stopped at Dunkin Donuts on the way to grab a sandwich and coffee. I wasn't about to be there with nothing on my stomach.

"Good morning." I spoke to everyone and put my things away so the overnight staff can fill me in on the patients.

"Can we get a nurse outside. A woman brought her son in claiming he suffered a seizure." Everyone looked at me because I'm the only 7-7 staff here so far. It was 6:45 so they were about to leave anyway.

"I'm going." I walked out in search of the woman and noticed the security guy picking a kid up from someone's car.

I held the door and asked if he were the one who had a seizure? She said yes and I had security bring him straight back. Usually a doctor would come out but like I said, shifts are changing and he's not in an active seizure now, so I'll handle the triage part before the doctor comes.

"Hey lil man. Not feeling good huh?" His eyes were barely open, but he shook his head no.

"I'm gonna be right outside calling my friend." I nodded and took the little boy's shirt off and passed him a gown. I placed the thermometer in his ear and noticed his fever was 103.2, which is enough to cause a seizure.

"I need some Tylenol in here right away and can one of you bring me the cart so I can do bloodwork?" I shouted out the door and kept my eye on the kid.

"Ok. He's on his way." His mom said and walked back in the room.

"How long has he had a fever?"

"He wasn't feeling well last night. I checked on him this morning and he was shaking; his eyes were rolling, and he had foam coming out his mouth." Another nurse came in with the cart and Tylenol.

"Did you call 911?" I asked.

"Did you see him pull up in an ambulance?" The woman got smart and me and the nurse Maria turned to look at her.

"Ma'am, I asked because some people contact 911 and leave. Then the ambulance is sitting at the house waiting for someone to open the door." I looked her up and down.

"And make that your last time getting smart with me. I'm trying to help your son." It took a lot outta me to remain calm. I understand she's probably scared for her son but no need her to snap on me.

"It's gonna hurt sweetie." After Maria gave him the Tylenol to bring the fever down, she held his arm while I took his blood.

"Good. My friend is here, and I don't think he'll be happy to know you got smart when you're supposed to be working." She walked out and I went to find her until Maria held me back.

"Who the fuck she think she is?" I whispered. Her son had fallen asleep and I didn't want him to hear me talking about his mom.

"Don't get yourself worked up. You know she must be miserable." We laughed.

"The hell you call me for, I ain't his daddy." I heard the voice and turned my head. I lifted the rail so the little boy wouldn't fall off.

"Stay here for a second." I told Maria. I didn't wanna walk out and the kid have a seizure and fall over.

"I'm not sure if I'll have a Co-pay or not and I don't get paid until Friday." This woman stood in front of Haven sobbing. Was he sleeping with her?

"Where the fuck is the money I gave you?" At this point everyone was staring.

"It was only two thousand and..." I cut her off.

"Haven you gave this woman two thousand dollars?" His eyes got big as hell.

"Yes he did and he gave me five before, not that it's your business. Why are you listening to our conversation?" All I could do is stare and he did the same.

"Haven why are you acting like we never slept together? It's been a year and..." The bitch was rubbing it in.

"You cheated on me?"

"Ariel." He reached out for me and I backed away.

"Cheated on her?" The girl covered her mouth like she said too much.

"Ariel?"

"Stop running Damien." I heard a lady shouting to her kid and didn't move fast enough. He ran straight to me and I fell face first on the ground.

Armonie

WAA! WAA! I rolled over to my son crying his head off. When I got off the phone with VJ, I ended up taking a nap with my son.

I looked down and his binky fell on the side of him. I placed it in his mouth, and he quieted down. I knew it wouldn't last long because he was wet and probably hungry.

After changing him, I picked my cell up and walked downstairs to get a bottle. As beautiful as the house is, I could do without all the steps. Granted, it's brand new and where VJ says we'd grow old in, but I may have to sleep downstairs when we older.

I fed my son, burped him, turned some baby show on and put him in the swing. I sat on the couch and picked my phone up to see if VJ called. When I noticed he didn't, it made my instincts kick in ASAP. He never goes an hour without calling and based on the time we hung up, it's been two. I didn't tell him I was taking a nap so it's not like he gave me time to sleep.

I called his phone and there was no answer. I dialed him again and again and still no one picked up. There's no way he wouldn't answer for me. My gut was telling me he's in trouble. I could go down there but I wouldn't know where the building was because he was in the hospital all that time. When he got out, he was home and then came here with me.

"Don't panic Monie. Don't work yourself up." I said to myself as I tried to think of what to do next.

"BRAYDEN!" I shouted to myself. I dialed him up quick.

"What up Monie?"

"When's the last time you spoke to VJ?" I asked already throwing some clothes on.

"Before he left for Virginia. Why?"

"Somethings wrong Brayden." I sat on the bed putting my sneakers on.

"WHAT?"

"I spoke to him the entire way to Virginia because he wouldn't let me go with him. He hung up to call Mycah and check on the office. I fell asleep and when I woke up, he still

31

hadn't called. Brayden, I called his phone back to back and it's no answer".”

"Shit." He cursed.

"I told him to let me go. Somethings wrong Brayden." I started crying.

"A'ight. I'm about to go down there."

"I'm coming." I was downstairs putting Legend in the car seat.

"Monie he's not going to want you there if..."

"NO! I'm going. I'm dropping Legend off to his mom, so I'll meet you over there." He blew his breath and agreed.

I still had VJ's bag packed from earlier so all I had to do was stick some clothes in it. I locked the door and strapped Legend in the back seat. I used the Bluetooth to call my dad.

"What's up?" He answered cheerfully.

"I'm going to Virginia with Brayden."

"For what?"

"VJ went down there because someone broke in his office. He hasn't called me or answered my calls. I can feel it daddy. Somethings wrong." I felt myself going into a panic.

"Ok. Hold on. Relax Monie and tell me what happened." I explained and he agreed somethings off. They knew how VJ felt about me and he would've definitely answered the phone.

"I'm calling Colby Jr and Jax. They'll go with y'all."

"Brayden's..." He cut me off.

"They're going. Whatever's going on may require more help."

"Ok." He hung up and called me back a few minutes later to say they're on the way to his house to meet me.

I stopped at a red light and reached behind to put Legend's binky in his mouth. He always wanted it but spit it out a lot too.

"Where you at now Armonie?"

"At the light on..."

KNOCK! KNOCK! I rolled my window down and sucked my teeth.

"What the fuck you want?"

"Who is that?" I heard my father asking through the Bluetooth.

"How the fuck are you alive? I thought I killed you."

Same day…

Armonie

"You thought you killed me?" I repeated the words Latifa said outside my window.

"Armonie who is that?" I could hear my father going off in the background.

"It was you outside the hospital?" She stood there with her arms folded and a smirk on her face.

"You don't deserve to be here. My brother suffered a lot at the hotel when your little boyfriend beat him up."

"Oh, the same boyfriend you tried to fuck but had his friend instead?" I gave her a disgusting look.

"You tried to kill me, because my man beat your brother up for hurting me. Yet, it was ok that Freddy almost killed me with the beatings?" She sucked her teeth.

"ARMONIE BANKS!" My father asked again but my focus was on the woman standing in front of me. I went to open the door and my son crying, stopped me.

WAA! WAA!

"Whose baby is that?" The bitch tried her hardest to see through the windows. The tint was extremely dark so she couldn't.

"Don't you worry about it." I told her.

BEEP! BEEP! Cars were honking for me to move out the way.

"Next time I'll make sure you die." She shouted before running to her car behind me.

I did the best thing for me and my son at the moment and that's pull off. I couldn't take the chance of beating her ass and someone jumping in my truck with my son, nor could I risk his life or VJ's, who no one knew right now if he were ok or not.

"I'm ok daddy."

"Who the fuck was that and she said something about being the one who tried to kill you." I blew my breath because I knew once he heard who it was, it's gonna be a problem.

"Freddy's sister."

"Say no more." The phone disconnected as I drove to VJ's parents house. His mom stepped out looking nervous.

36

"He's going to be fine Monie." She hugged me and walked around to get Legend. His father stepped out and so did Brayden, and VJ's other brother Valley. Yea it's a lotta V's in their family.

"I'm driving with Monie." I turned and saw Vanity getting out a brand-new Bentley truck.

"Ugh, we driving your truck." I pointed and started laughing

"You have no idea the amount of gifts Antoine showered me with." She said smiling. This woman was deeply in love with her man. I thought I had it bad for VJ, but she had me beat.

"Why?"

"Because now that I'm here, he wants to get married and have kids." She smiled as she continued talking.

"Damn Girl. You strung his ass all the way out." I said checking out the truck.

"You got my brother the same." And it hit me again that he's missing.

"Shit. I have to pick my brother and cousin up. Y'all ready?" I asked, kissed my son and all of us jumped in our rides.

"I found out who tried to kill me." Vanity snapped her neck to look at me.

"Latifa."

"Latifa?" She asked confused.

"Freddy's sister."

"Get the hell outta here." I shook my head

"Nope. I couldn't find out anything from her because Legend was in the truck and I rushed to get here. But don't worry. When we get VJ, I'm coming back for her." I spoke firm about getting Freddy's sister.

She's never liked me and I have no idea why nor could I care less. She's one of the women who knew her brother had a hand problem and sat back watching. Never intervening and basically blamed me for getting him angry. It's sad when a woman can watch another suffer and not do anything about it.

"Damn." I said and saw the few cars in front of my parents' house.

"What?"

"We going down there deep." I stepped out and everyone started coming out the house. Brayden pulled in behind me.

"Monie, I think you should stay here." My mom said and walked towards me.

"I can't mommy. I need to see for myself he's ok."

"You sure because his family's going and so are your brothers and cousins." She pointed to the other cars.

"Yes. I'll be careful. I promise." She hugged me.

"Let's go." Colby Jr said and walked over with his best friend Nayquan.

"Hey sis." He embraced me in a bear hug, and I introduced him to Vanity. He licked his lips.

"She's taken."

"Don't be a hater." Vanity joked.

"I don't wanna hear Antoine mouth."

"Antoine? Oh, you lil Tech woman?" He put his hands up.

"I said the same thing. It's a small world, right?" Colby Jr laughed, and they walked to their cars.

"Antoine know you going?" I asked.

"Hell no. He would've made me stay, while he went." She started cracking up.

Vanity continued calling VJ's phone on the ride there and it's still no answer, which made me worry again. It's getting late and I was nervous we wouldn't be able to track him. We don't have bloodhound dogs like cops. Yea, I watch too much criminal minds.

"How are you Monie?" Vanity asked and turned the radio down.

"What you mean?"

"It hasn't been long since you were in the hospital."

"I'm ok. Taking care of myself, VJ and Legend is taking a toll on me, but I'm ok." All I could think of is her brother at the moment.

"You need a vacation. I'm talking about the kind where you, my nephew and brother cut off the world and relax."

"I would love it but right now we can't." She tried to ask me more questions on my reason, but my mind was only on VJ.

Four hours later we were crossing into Virginia. Vanity gave me directions on where to go and another half hour later, we were at the condominiums where the main office was. There is one in every condo, but this is the one they kept the money in.

We glanced around and the sun had gone down, and the condos looked deserted besides people walking around their places. VJ's car was there along with someone else's.

KNOCK! KNOCK! I rolled the window down for my brother.

"Don't get out until I come get you."

"But..."

"You heard me." He said in a firm tone and I listened.

All of them walked up to the office slowly, when outta nowhere you saw someone come out with a shotgun or something. Everyone drew their weapons.

"That's Mycah." Vanity hopped out with me behind. Fuck that staying in the truck shit.

"Vanity?" He questioned.

"Yes. Where's my brother?" He put the gun down and it took a minute for everyone else to do the same, but they did eventually.

"What happened?"

"I don't know. VJ called and said he was coming because something happened. I told him to call when he's here, but I fell asleep. I woke up to his text saying he's in town but by the time I got here, the place was empty. I mean Ashley here looking like someone beat her to death." We all ran inside, and the office was beyond fucked up. You could tell a robbery took place.

"You ok?" Vanity asked Ashley who sat in the corner with her knees pulled to her chest. Her eye was swollen, and she couldn't stop crying.

"Why isn't she at a hospital?" Vanity questioned Mycah since he was already here.

"Mannn, she don't wanna go." All of us stepped over stuff and I noticed Vanity tryna clean up.

"Brayden go through the security footage." He walked over to where she pointed which was a small door and went in.

"Has anyone seen Monie or Monee, I'm not sure how to say her name." Ashley asked.

"I'm Monie." I made my way to her.

"VJ said he knew you'd come for him, that's why he loves you." I smiled and kneeled down in front of her.

"Is he ok?"

"I don't know. The person had five or six guys with him. They came in and attacked him." I started getting upset listening.

"He was laid out on the ground bleeding. Monie his last words before they snatched him out was, tell my girl to check my location."

"Check his location? What does that mean?" I paced the floor tryna think of what he meant.

"Where's your phone?" My brother asked and snatched it out my hand. He went to find friends on the iPhone and ran over to Mycah.

"Where's this?" Colby asked pointing to something on my phone

"A house in the hood. I mean it's nothing but street niggas out there. VJ would never go there because they stay shooting and..." Mycah stopped talking.

"What?" I asked.

"If they took him there it means they're either gonna kill him or beat him up so bad, he'll wish he were dead." Mycah ran his hand down his face.

"But they already fought him from what she says." I pointed to Ashley getting helped off the floor. I felt bad because she's a property manager and probably never experienced anything like this.

"The street dudes over there don't take kind to outsiders, and even though VJ has lived here damn near all his life, they don't know him. They may think he's tryna sell on their territory. Fuck! We have to get over there."

"Look at this shit." All of us ran in the small room Brayden sat in looking at the footage.

It showed people in masks come in to rob the place the night before. The next day Ashley arrived, called the cops and then VJ. Hours later you see VJ get there, somebody walking in and VJ's facial expression showed he was shocked. At first none of us could see who the person was until they started fighting.

"That's not who I think it is." Colby and Jax both said at the same time.

"No way." I looked closer to the screen.

"FREDDY!" I shouted. *What the fuck?*

VJ

"Why the fuck you bring him here?" I heard some dude yelling in the other room.

This punk motherfucker Freddy showed up at the condos and I was shocked to say the least. He started popping shit, and in the process, I sent my location to Monie's phone. His dumb ass went out to his car or something so I turned my ringer off and down so if she called, no one would hear the vibration. When it's quiet you can hear everything. I'm glad I did because his punk ass had some dudes come jump me.

Anyway, I knew my ride or die fiancé would figure out something's wrong because that's how she is. Always worried about everyone else instead of herself. When I get outta here I'm gonna take her away. We both need a long vacation.

I don't know how long I've been here because these niggas tied me up and tossed me in some truck, after hitting me over the head with something. I managed to get out the rope they had around me, which was loose as hell. You can tell they're amateurs.

46

I would've jumped out the window already, had bars not been on it. All I could assume is we were in the hood. One place, I never came to, except to pick Mecca up from her sisters and the time I saw Lily.

"I know how boss is about outsiders and..." Some guy said.

BAM! I heard and limped to the door.

"Yo! Why you hit me?" This Freddy dude is a nuisance wherever he goes.

"Boss is here." Somebody yelled out and all of them got quiet. Whoever dude was had these idiots shook. The door opened and in he walked with someone else.

"You've got to be fucking shitting me." I said to myself and shook my head.

"Tha fuck going on here?" I watched as all the guys remained quiet. All of the guys looked as if they were gonna shit on themselves.

"Freddy what you doing down in this neck of the woods? You from Jersey."

"He mad because I stole his girl and had me jumped at my office." I was leaning on the door and you could tell how surprised they were, to know I knew their boss.

"VJ?" Antoine and Marco Jr. questioned at the same time. I walked slowly to where they were.

"Hold the fuck up. You called me from Jersey saying some nigga was down here tryna move in on your territory. He's gonna sell product which may cause the cops to look into my operation and the whole time you were talking about VJ." No one said a word. Marco walked up on some guy.

"Ain't that what you said Bradshaw?" Marco asked and they all stood there quiet.

"Bradshaw?" I laughed.

"We didn't know. Freddy called and told us about this guy." Marco and Antoine stared at Freddy.

"Which one of y'all motherfuckers did this?" They pointed to me. I couldn't see how I looked but I damn sure felt bad. I probably had a black eye; my ribs may be cracked and a few bruises here and there but otherwise; I'm good.

"No one knows now huh?" Antoine barked pulling out his gun and placing a silencer on it.

See Marco Jr. took over his father's empire and like best friends do, Antoine hopped on board with him. People feared both of them in Jersey and should, because between these two and the reaper, it's best you stay away from them.

I may not fuck with Haven but his name rings bells on the street. Brayden told me about him a long time ago but I didn't remember because I barely visited Jersey. And regardless if people only know the reaper, they're well aware of his sidekick, which is my cousin.

"They did it." Some guy shouted and pointed to the four guys next to him and Freddy.

"I hate a snitch." Antoine said and shook his head.

PHEW! Dudes head blew off. What kind of bullets is he using?

"Next." Antoine went down the line.

"Come over here Freddy." Marco said and as much as I wanted to watch Antoine kill these niggas, I needed to see what he'd do to this punk. He pulled him over to the corner.

49

"Why don't you like VJ?" He pointed to me getting close. Freddy remained quiet.

"I can't hear you." Marco put his hand behind his ear pretending he had to extend it to hear.

"He came to Jersey, took my girl and attacked me like three times. He needs to die." Freddy turned to me.

"Yo! You sound like a bitch right now." Marco looked him up and down.

"A woman can't be stolen from a nigga unless she wants to be. Were you fighting her? Cheating? What? How was he able to take her?"

"Tell him how you beat on her. How you cheated numerous times and threatened to kill her if she left. How you're mad she has my son and we're about to get married?"

"Monie ain't have no kid. She may not be a virgin anymore, but she doesn't have a kid."

POW! I used all the energy I had and hooked off.

"Don't be telling my girl business." I stared down at him on the ground.

50

"I can't wait until my sister finds Monie and finishes her off. You don't deserve her..." I grabbed him up by his shirt.

"What you say?"

"You heard me. My sister did that to her because of you putting me in the hospital." He had a dumb smirk on his face. How the fuck he ok beating on Monie, but can't nobody whoop his ass?

"WHAT?" I don't know what happened, but my Incredible Hulk strength kicked in and I started beating his ass. I couldn't feel any pain as the adrenaline rushed through me. All I could think of is how Monie got snatched out the car and all the scars left on her body from the stab wounds.

"Damn." Antoine said after pulling me off. Freddy was damn near dead.

"Can I get your gun?" I asked Antoine and he handed it right over. I wasted no time taking Freddy's life and couldn't wait to get his sister.

"Get someone here ASAP and tell Raheem to meet me at the club tonight. I may have to change his position." I turned to Marco.

51

"Raheem who?" I asked him when he hung up. When he mentioned the same dude Mia cheated on me with, I told him he's next.

"Damn nigga. Now I gotta find someone else."

"I think he's hiding Mecca and if he is, then I'm getting rid of him. Matter of fact, can you take me to his spot?"

"Man, if my girl gets mad at me for being here longer than I said, you're dealing with her mouth." I busted out laughing because Monie be on the same shit.

"Yo, your sister know what's going on?" Antoine asked.

"If she with Monie, I have no doubt she'll be here too." I had a grin on my face. Monie was hardheaded when it came to me, so I know she's here, or on her way.

"I'ma fuck her up. Is Monie in town?"

"I don't know yet. But if she is, nine times outta ten so is Vanity." I told him.

"Watch this." He called Vanity up and she answered.

"Hey babe. I'm with Monie out eating." Vanity said as soon as she picked up.

"Oh yea." Vanity lied her ass off.

52

"Yea. I'll bring you something home so when you get back from Virginia, it'll be there." He laughed.

"A'ight." He hung up without hearing Vanity out. Two seconds later, his phone rung back. He let her go to voicemail just as a shitload of cars pulled in with Jersey plates.

"Damn VJ. Your girl ain't playing about you." Marco said and laughed. Monie stepped out the truck and ran straight to me.

"Get out the truck Vanity." Antoine yelled and she didn't move. I swore, I heard the doors lock.

"Out to eat huh?" Monie shrugged her shoulders

"I told her to tell him. Are you ok? I was so worried. I told you to bring me." She checked over my body and had me walk to the truck.

"We need to find Freddy." Monie said.

"He's gone ma." She turned to me.

"What you mean?"

"He's never gonna bother you again." Tears fell down her face.

"You are always saving me."

"This time you saved me; well you were going to." We started kissing until everyone told us to get a room.

"Marco, I'm gonna stay a few days to get better. Can we deal with Raheem then?" I asked because I really needed to rest and I wanted to be the one to take him and Mecca out.

"He's having a party, or some shit this weekend, so we'll be back."

"He making that kind of money?" This nigga had local celebrities coming to his party and everything from what his flyer said, that Marco just showed me.

"He's a corner boy. He barely makes shit and must've come into money." I stared at Monie.

"You think he robbed you?" She asked.

"Now that I think of it, Yup. Mecca is the only one who knew that safe was there. Shit, Mycah didn't know and he's my boy. I have no doubt she set it up. Let me get to the hospital to get meds and get better. I have four days to recuperate before I get him. I know the best way to start after the hospital."

"You know I got you." She smiled and unlocked the door. Antoine took Vanity out and I sat down.

"I'm happy you're ok babe." Monie said and we all pulled off.

"I'm not leaving my family anytime soon." She leaned over and kissed me.

"You better not."

"Where's Legend?" I asked and don't know why I bothered looking in the back seat. I know she wouldn't bring him when she had no idea what was going on.

"Your mom has him. Oh, make sure you call her. She was very worried."

"I will right after I make love to my fiancé." She smiled hard as I gave her the directions to the hospital.

Three hours later, I was discharged with a few bruised ribs, a black eye and scrapes and bruises like I thought. The doctor gave me some pain medicine and told me to take it easy. I'ma take it easy alright.

"Meet me in the bedroom." Monie said walking into the hotel suite. She didn't wanna stay at one of the empty condos because there wasn't any furniture in them.

"I'll be right there." I sent a text to my parents and told Vanity to have Antoine go with her to straighten up the office. When she text back ok, I stripped out my clothes, took a shower and met Monie in the bedroom. It hurt like hell when we finished but the sex and medication put me straight to sleep.

Haven

"Yo, if anything wrong with my girl, I'm fucking you up." I told Sharika who stood there pretending as if she didn't know who Ariel was. Every bitch out here knew who she was because like Marlena said, Ariel's page is open and its pictures of us on it.

Not only that, she's already made me aware of her stalkerish ways on IG. Hell, she's stalking whoever her baby daddy girl is now, so I know she's been all over Ariel's page.

"Haven, I didn't know." I wanted to smack the shit outta her.

"Get the fuck out my face bitch." I walked behind the stretcher Ariel was on.

See, I made plans to apologize to my cousin and try and be cordial with her man. Unfortunately, I fell asleep and when I woke up, Ariel was gone. Then, Sharika calls me crying and carrying on about something happening to her son. Asking me to come up and sit with her until they find out what's wrong. I told her ass HELL NO.

The only reason I even came to the hospital is to see Ariel and tell her I was going to Armonie's house. She's not allowed to use her phone at work. Plus, I wanted to tell her we still a couple.

I'm a fucked up nigga but I don't play when it comes to mine; which is why I cursed Sharika out. Ariel didn't know who to believe and I couldn't tell her the truth because somebody's bad ass kid was running around. I can't say in the hallway because it wasn't one. It's the area in front of the nurse's desk and between the rooms.

Anyway, when the little bastard knocked my girl over, I screamed on him. He pissed himself and I didn't care. I rolled Ariel over and blood was coming out her nose and she had tears falling down her face. I lifted her up and a nurse brought the stretcher to me. Now we're on the baby floor watching the nurse put monitors on her belly.

"Haven." Ariel grabbed my hand, squeezed it and closed her eyes. I think she was scared they'd say something was wrong with the baby. I was too but I had to be strong for her just in case.

BMMBPP! BMMBPP! You heard clear as day.

"What's that?" I asked.

"Her baby's heartbeat. The doctors gonna want to do an internal exam and ultrasound to make sure everything's ok. How's your nose Ariel?" The nurse asked. It wasn't bleeding bad, but she did hit it. They were able to stick a cotton ball in to clog it.

"It hurts."

"And your arm?" I looked down at the one she recently had the cast taken off of and it looked fine.

"It's ok. My ankle hurts tho." I let go of her hand, removed the clog shoes she had on, then her sock."

"GOT DAMN." I didn't mean to scare her, but it was swollen.

"What's wrong?"

"Nothing Ariel. It looks like a small fracture. Who are you sir?" The nurse asked with an attitude.

"Your worst got damn nightmare if you don't fix your face." She looked at Ariel who was shaking her head.

"You better tell her Ariel." I wasn't playing. Who this bitch thought she was questioning me?

"It's ok. He's worried about me." She tried to diffuse the situation, but the bitch kept going.

"Ok but he..."

"Bitch, I will knock your teeth out if you say anything smart. Matter of fact, beat it. She doesn't need negative people around her." The nurse looked at me.

"Please go. I'll wait for the doctor to come in." Ariel pleaded with her to leave, where I could care less because I'll knock her out. The nurse rolled her eyes and I started walking behind her.

"HAVEN!" Ariel shouted. The nurse turned around.

"She just saved your life bitch." I slammed the door.

"You have to work on your temper." I waved her off and sat on the side of the bed.

"How could you cheat on me?"

"I swear on my mom, I didn't. When she said it's been a year, she's kind of right." Ariel sucked her teeth.

"I messed around with her the last year Juicy and I were together but not with you. Marlena is the only person I slipped up with and you weren't my girl yet, so you really can't count that." She threw the tissue box at me.

"The day I made you my girl, I have not slept with anyone else."

"Why were you giving her money?" I blew my breath in the air and explained Sharika's situation. I didn't wanna tell her business, but I had to tell Ariel. I ain't want her to think I'm taking care of other bitches.

"I knew her son looked familiar."

"You know the daddy?" I asked giving her the side eye.

"No but I feel like I may. It's as if his face is the exact same as someone I've been around. I can't explain it."

"You sound crazy." I told her.

"I'm serious Haven. Have you ever seen someone and been like, I've seen them before? It's the same with the kid, only I saw an older version. It'll come to me eventually."

"How are you Ariel?" The doctor asked walking in with the same nurse.

"Hell no. That bitch got an attitude and is very negative. Send someone else." The doctor sent her out and another nurse came in

"Ok. Let's see what we have going on." He did an internal exam which I didn't care for and expressed my ignorance. He laughed and so did Ariel. The other nurse stood quiet as a mouse.

The doctor said our baby was fine, apologized for the other nurse, and told us we could go in an hour. Her ankle was badly bruised and swollen. They put an air cast on it, gave her crutches and said she didn't really need it but to have them in case.

By the time we got home, it was one in the afternoon. Her parents were at the door and I took a seat on the couch. Well her father had me follow him outside to talk as he says. He told Ariel to lay down and relax. She tried to come outside but he forbid it. I need that kinda control over her because she damn sure wouldn't have listened if I said it.

"Have a seat Haven." He pointed to the patio set on Ariel's porch. I must say she picked out a nice ass house and decorated it nice too.

I sat and asked if he mind me rolling a blunt. I've never had to sit with a chick's father and I need to calm myself because my temper can get outta control. I don't need Ariel holding out on the pussy because she mad. Mr. Glover cool as hell and yes, I've known him forever but its different now because I'm with his daughter.

"What's the problem with you and my nephew?" I shifted my eyes to where he stood. I thought we were gonna discuss Ariel and he bringing up this nigga.

"What you mean?" I focused back on the task of rolling my blunt.

"Don't play games with me. It's bad enough my son is your best friend and y'all doing some serial killer shit."

"We are right?" I started laughing.

"Now you're with my daughter, she's pregnant and I don't even wanna begin to think if my grandchild will be like you or Brayden."

"Grandkids." I corrected him.

"What?"

"You said grandchild and I said grandkids. Ariel having all eight of my kids." I said with conviction.

"Eight?"

"Unless you want her to have ten." I shrugged my shoulders.

"However many kids you want ain't gonna happen if you can't make amends with her cousin." I went to speak but he cut me off.

"Regardless of him swinging off on you first at the restaurant, you need to respect him standing up for her, the same as you do for Armonie. Now y'all dealt with the restaurant issue, him and your cousin fell in love, have a baby, are about to get married and what do you do? Go and ruin their happiness because you can't be quiet around him." He sat across from me.

"How would you feel if your daughter came and said her boyfriend's cousins did all that to her."

"Well first of all, I'm not having girls and if I do, she can't have a boyfriend until she thirty. That's settled." I lit the blunt.

"Are you from this planet?" He asked with a serious face.

"Sometimes I ask myself the same question." I blew smoke out and stared in the sky.

"Look, I'm not here to lecture you but he's my nephew and nobody in my family or yours feel like dealing with your attitude or smart mouth at family functions. You're either gonna stay quiet, or I'm telling Ariel you not only cheated on her but got another bitch pregnant. That's settled." He slammed his hand down on the table and snatched the blunt out my hand.

"She won't believe you."

"Ariel knows her daddy won't lie to her." He had a grin on his face. I stared at this man and knew he was right.

"You wouldn't do that."

"Try me." He blew smoke and started coughing a little.

"What kind of weed is this?"

"The kind yo old ass shouldn't be smoking." I tried to snatch it away and he moved back.

"I doubt we'll ever be cool, but I'll stay quiet from now on. And I'm telling Ariel what you said."

"Never in a million years would I think you'd be a snitch." He said and I had to laugh.

"Hell yea I'm snitching to her about that. What if you really do it and she try and leave me?" I thought about it.

"You know what. I'm not gonna tell her and when she comes up missing because you lied, don't get mad." This time I snatched the blunt and took a pull.

"Haven did you eat today?" Ariel's mom peeked out asking.

"No. Your daughter didn't feed me." Her mom loved me since we were kids too.

"Ariel Glover. How can you not feed him?" I heard her yell and shut the sliding door.

"Snitching ass nigga." Her pops said and finished the blunt with me.

When we got inside, Ariel's parents left to go to the store because Mrs. Glover said she's making us dinner. I couldn't wait. Her mom can cook her ass off.

Ariel

"Haven watch my foot." I whispered as he slid me to the edge of the bed and dove in.

"Ssss. Fuck!" I gripped the sheets, arched my back and came hard. This is the first time he and I had sex since the melee at his grandmother's dinner.

"I'm about to put another baby in you." I laughed at his silliness.

Haven gets on everyone nerves; including mine but we have more good days then bad. Actually, they're always good except the time I caught him in the office getting head and when he's bothering VJ.

"I love you Haven and I want us to work but you have to stop. Oh shit..." He hit a certain spot to make me lose my voice.

"You like that huh?" I nodded and bit down on my lip.

"Yesss. Oh God yes." My legs started shaking and he didn't stop there. Haven had me in every position possible as long as it didn't affect my foot.

"Ah shit Ariel." He let go and collapsed on the side of me. He used his index finger to turn my head towards him.

"I love you too and I'll try and be a good man to you." I gently kissed his lips.

"You know the type of man I am so don't expect miracles. I won't cheat on you and I'm always gonna have your back."

"I don't want you perfect Haven because then I'll be bored." He started laughing.

"I fell in love with the aggressive, arrogant, ignorant, serial killing reaper and I only want you to be who you are."

"Why I gotta be all that?" He smiled.

"It's who you are baby and I love it. Just stay away from VJ and he'll do the same."

"Why does he keep coming up?"

"Because you two are the reason things are hectic within the families. Oh, and you still need to apologize to Monie." I picked my phone up and sent her a message to call me. I haven't spoken to her in two days, which is weird. I put the phone down, got as close to Haven as I could and fell asleep.

****

RING! RING! I answered my phone on the nightstand. "Hello."

"Umm. Hello, I'm trying to reach Haven." I looked at the phone and realized it was his and the name read Sharika.

"Sharika, I'm not sure why you're still contacting him when he's told you on various occasions, he has someone." I felt Haven's arm on my stomach.

"I know but my son..."

"Your son has a father Sharika and frankly I don't appreciate you tryna force him off on my man. And then you're asking him for money. Money that's only for me and our future kids." I sat up.

"I understand but he's been here in the last two days and I'm not sure what he told you, but we've been intimate and..." Haven snatched the phone out my hand.

"And bitch you better run because when I find you, I'm gonna cut your got damn throat for lying." He hung up and turned on his back.

"I know you weren't with her." He had his arm across his face.

"Not the point Ariel. What if you didn't know? The bitch has to go. I don't need her stressing you out." I smiled and kissed his chest.

"This is what happens when you give these women what I get."

"Ssss." He silently moaned when I kissed above his hairline.

"No one has ever gotten what you did, not even Juicy. Shit Ariel." I spit on the tip and flicked my tongue in and out the slit.

"Her pussy nowhere near good as yours and we barely fucked. She has good conversation and decent head, that's it. Got damn." I swallowed him whole and made him remember why I'm the best.

"We need a shower." I told him after he let me taste him. Last night we went straight to bed after sex.

After we got out and put clothes on, I called Armonie back since she responded.

"Hey boo." I Face Timed her instead. She was lying in bed but it wasn't her bed.

"Hey. Hold on. VJ sleeping." She pulled the covers off and walked out the room.

"Where are you?" I asked.

"Virginia."

"Virginia?" Haven questioned. I didn't even know he was in the room.

"Is that my cousin?" I gave her a *duh* look.

"You know ain't no other man here." She laughed.

"I forgot you're with the reaper." She put her hand up in quotes.

"Anyway. Why you in Virginia?" She started explaining and I could see aggravation on Haven's face.

"Then, Latifa admitted to being the one who tried to kill me." That shocked me.

"WHAT?" Haven jumped up and started pacing the room.

"When we were getting ready to come here, she jumped out her car at a stoplight." Armonie told us.

"Was Legend with you?" Haven asked and Armonie shook her head yes.

"I'm gonna kill her whole family." He grabbed his keys and I grabbed his wrist.

"Calm down Haven." I didn't need him being reckless when everyone is outta town. He can take care of himself, but I still wanted him to stay in.

"Freddy's dead."

"How?" She turned her head and smiled.

"My fiancé did it." He leaned down and kissed her.

"Hey cuz." He spoke and went to the bathroom. I could see how slow he moved.

"He's gonna be fine Ariel." I guess she noticed how upset it made me to see him like that.

"After we go to this party tomorrow, we'll be back and hopefully all this will be over."

73

"What party?" Haven asked and we listened to her explain some plan they had to get this Raheem guy and Mecca.

"I'm not comfortable with you going Armonie." Haven voiced his concern and I had to agree.

"He doesn't want me to go either but I'm going." She folded her arms and I could see VJ in the background shaking his head.

"Did you take the medicine?" Armonie asked and left the phone on the table to get it for him.

"I'm not taking it tomorrow Monie. It makes me drowsy."

"VJ."

"I need to be alert Monie and even if I take it in the morning, the effects are still too much."

"You know it's a no-win situation." I told her and she started laughing.

"I know and he's right. I can't have him getting hurt again."

"No, he can't." I said.

"So how are you and my cousin doing?" She asked and I turned the camera to Haven who was rolling a blunt.

"Fine."

"Good. I'm excited for my new baby cousin to come." She was all smiles and I saw Haven doing the same. I loved how she didn't hold a grudge towards Haven, but I knew she would let him have it in person.

"Let me get off the phone Armonie. I promised my mom she could come to the doctors with us today."

"I thought you saw the baby already."

"I did but it was because I fell. My actual doctor's appointment is today."

"Ok. Call me later. I need to take care of VJ."

"Yes you do." I heard him say.

"Bye." I hung up and saw Haven with a blunt hanging out his mouth and packing a suitcase.

"Where you going?"

"We're going to Virginia."

"Huh?"

75

"After the doctor's appointment, we're going because if something happens to her nigga, she'll never be the same."

"Wait! You're going to help VJ?" He turned around.

"Correction. I'm making sure my cousin will be straight." I put my head down smiling. He won't say it, but I think this is his way of making up for the shit he's done. I just hope this ends all the drama.

Mecca

"I'm finally about to get my position babe." Raheem spoke as we stripped to get in the shower. He was having a party tonight for his birthday and after he robbed VJ, he had more than enough money to ball out.

The day of the robbery, I was nervous because he's never robbed anyone to my knowledge and scared because what it something went wrong? Him and the two guys drove there in a black van at night and broke in. Well they broke in the office and I gave him the code to shut the alarm off. VJ trusted me not to pay attention I guess, so I've known the code for a very long time.

Anyway, Raheem told me they found the safe, set the small bomb off and it opened. He said there were checks, money orders and tons of cash. I remember VJ saying not everyone had bank accounts and others only wanted to pay in cash. With four or five sets of condos, and over 100 units each, I'd say they made off with a lot an that's just the money in Virginia. He had condos in Maryland too.

He had me count it and it was over seventy thousand. Once he split it between the three of them, he passed me off five to get a complete makeover. I mean, he had me purchase different color eye contacts, wigs and he made me lose weight. I wasn't fat but my face being smaller did make me look different. His thing was for me to go out places with him and I couldn't without a change.

I even stopped by my mother's one day to see if she noticed a difference, and at first, she had no idea who I was. That alone made it believable.

"Your position?" I questioned opening the shower curtain.

"Marco Jr. called and mentioned a higher position opening and he's interviewing for the spot."

"Marco Jr.?" I heard that name before but I can't remember where.

"He's from Jersey."

"Oh ok." We finished washing up and stepped out the shower.

Forty minutes later, I was dressed in a strapless black dress, with some Christie Louboutin shoes, pocketbook to match, hair and nails done with my gray eyes and I even wore one of those bull nose rings to throw people off.

"You real sexy Mecca." He licked his lips and ran his hands over my ass.

"So are you." He had on a nice suit with cold cuff links and gator shoes. He brought some big diamond earrings and a nice chain to match. We were gonna be the baddest couple in there and no one could spoil our night.

DING DONG! I looked at Raheem.

"It's Lily."

"Except her." I haven't spoken or seen her since she fought me.

"Be nice." I rolled my eyes.

"Hey cuz. You look nice." I couldn't front. Lily by all means is a bad bitch and her outfit was fire. Didn't leave much to imagination but still nice.

"Who this?" Raheem smirked.

"Mecca." Lily looked at me again.

79

"Hmph. I guess no one will recognize her. You ready?" She ignored my presence the rest of the way and vice versa.

When we pulled up to the club it was semi packed, and a line was forming. The night I met VJ's cousin in the club, it was packed and people were still tryna get in. Mind you it wasn't a party; yet the place was jumping. This will have to do because I really can't take the chance of anyone noticing me.

Raheem helped me out the limo he rented, and we walked in like the stars we were.

"It's the birthday dude himself with two beautiful women on his arm. We know one is the infamous Lily but the other must be from outta town. Happy Birthday Rah." The DJ said and I smiled. The DJ was cool with VJ so if he didn't recognize me either, I did a great job.

Security led us upstairs to where he had a VIP section. It had mad bottles and the two dudes who robbed my ex's spot were there already with strippers on their lap.

I found a seat at the circular table and poured myself a drink. Lily left the area and I saw her speaking to some guy on the dance floor I never seen before. She had her hand sliding

80

under his shirt until he snatched her wrist. He must've been gripping it tight because her facial expression was changing. I sat there watching and never said a word to Raheem. The guy can break her wrist for all I care.

"OH SHIT Y'ALL. JERSEY IN THE MOTHERFUCKING HOUSE! MY NIGGA VJ HERE AND I MUST SAY HIS WOMAN IS, GOT DAMN SHE BAD!" The DJ shouted. Raheem and I both leaned over the banister.

"That's his girl?" Raheem asked dripping in envy. I can't front. The Armonie bitch had all the women in here beat; including Lily. I never paid attention to her in Jersey but she was beautiful. I can see why he fell for her but then again, VJ isn't all about looks. I watched in lust as his sexy ass spoke to the DJ.

"My bad y'all, the woman on his arm is his fiancé. So, all y'all niggas can look but don't touch." VJ smiled and leaned in to kiss her.

"Clearly it's his fiancé." I said dripping with sarcasm.

"Don't worry babe. A few more months, I'm gonna hit that spot again and buy you the biggest ring ever." Him saying

81

that made me look and even from the distance we were at, the bitch's ring was big and shiny.

"Who the hell is that?" One of the dudes said and we looked to see other niggas walking in. They were deep as hell. A few of their faces I remembered from Jersey, which meant they weren't really here for leisure.

"We need to go."

"What? Its my party Mecca. I'm not leaving because they came."

"Raheem look at them. There's no way they came to party."

"You worry too much. Sit in the corner with me real quick." I put my glass down, walked over to where he was, straddled him and slid right down. I didn't wear panties for this purpose.

We already spoke about having sex in the club and here we are doing it. VJ would've never allowed this to happen. He was too nervous someone would see what he had at home. It makes me wonder if I should look at it the same.

"You almost done?" I heard and felt Raheem grab my waist. His voice sent chills up my spine and if I had a dick, it would've went soft.

"What's up VJ?" I never turned around and Raheem smirked.

"I'ma let you finish and we'll talk. And if I were you, I'd cover my girl's ass." I pulled my dress down a little and put my face in his neck.

"How did he get passed security?" I questioned because we were the only people in this section.

"I don't know. Let me see what he wants." I lifted up and sat on the side after pulling my dress all the way down. He fixed his clothes and stepped over to where VJ was. I couldn't help but be petty and walk past his girl. VJ had his hand intertwined with hers as he spoke to Raheem.

"Nice shoes." She said and I kept walking. I went in the bathroom and returned to see the situation began escalating. VJ had Raheem bent over backwards on the balcony. No one moved and his cousin Brayden stood by his side.

"What are you doing VJ?" Lily asked and tried to pry his hands off. I watched Armonie tap Lily on the shoulder and tell her to back up.

"This my cousin. Fuck that."

"I'm asking you nicely." Lily looked her up and down and Armonie laughed in her face. Two seconds later, she had Lily on the floor bashing her head in it.

"Ok Armonie." VJ let Raheem go and all you heard was screaming as his body hit the dance floor below. While all the commotion was going on, I slipped out the door.

"Hey sexy." I turned to see a guy who looked familiar, but I couldn't place him. He had a blunt hanging out his mouth with his leg against the wall. He was sexy himself.

"You tryna bounce or what?" I focused on the people running out the club, back to him and back to the club again.

"Why not?" He reached his hand out for me. It wasn't until we dipped in a different area that I realized he was the guy who Lily tried to seduce earlier.

"This you?" I asked about the Dodge Charger in front of us.

"Yup." He opened the door, helped me in and after sitting on the driver's side, pulled off.

"You hungry?" He asked.

"Kinda." I kept checking the rear-view mirror.

"A'ight. My people's girl enjoys cooking. We about to hit them up." I nodded and laid my head back.

"You seemed stressed." He said and continued driving. This man was sexy as hell and I couldn't help but get turned on. The liquor probably enhanced my sexual desire but who cares?

"What's your name?"

"Mec... I mean Megan." He picked his ringing cell up and asked the person if the food was ready.

"Cool." He responded and hung up. We drove for about twenty minutes before pulling up at a spot I knew all too well.

"Umm. I think we're at the wrong place." No other cars were here and it was dark as hell.

"Nah. This is the spot my peoples at." He pulled in VJ's parents old house.

"You know who lives here?"

"Yea. They recently moved here." I finally let out the breath I was holding in. If they recently moved here, it can't be his parents. Then, I remembered Raheem saying VJ's entire family moved to Jersey.

"Oh ok." I opened the door and waited for him to get out.

"You a bad bitch tho." He said walking behind me.

"Huh?"

"I'm just saying Mecca. I hate when bad bitches get caught up and lose their life behind dumb shit." I tried to run when he said my name and he wrapped his hand around my hair. Somehow, I tripped and he began dragging me to the door. I could scream but VJ's parents old house was in a secluded area. The neighbors were a mile away.

"Please let me go. Who are you?" I tried to pry his hands off but his grip was serious.

"Oh. I forgot to introduce myself." He lifted me up by my hair smiling.

"I'm the motherfucking reaper." I knew then this was it for me.

VJ

"So you thought I wouldn't find out you robbed me?" I stared into the crowd below as Raheem tried to find the words to lie. I wasn't sure who broke in my office until Monie reminded me Mecca could've told him the information.

At first, I assumed it was Freddy since he had the audacity to show his face down here. But low and behold, this punk ass nigga is the one.

"Ain't nobody rob you." He said and tried to wave me off. I felt Monie squeezing my hand as she told someone they had on nice shoes. I let go and stared Raheem in his face.

"Ok. You didn't rob me. Where's Mecca?"

"I don't know." I chuckled.

"You're willing to lose your life over a bitch?" I asked to see what he'd say.

"She's not a bitch and I'm not telling you shit." He backed up fixing his cuff links.

"A'ight then." I hooked off and held him over the banister. Lily was screaming for me to stop until Monie got her.

Raheem begged me to lift him up, but I couldn't. Not only did he rob me, but he was hiding Mecca.

"Any last request?" I asked as he tried grabbing onto the banister.

"Please let me up." He begged and even cried. I let go and watched Raheem's neck break as he hit the floor. Oh well. He should've never lied about robbing me and gave up Mecca's whereabouts.

"You good?" I checked Monie over after she whooped Lily's ass and we got outside. People were running around, while others stayed around being nosy.

"I'm fine." She smiled. We were walking down the street from the club about to leave.

"Do you think he got her?" I asked about Colby Jr going to Raheem's place and getting Mecca.

"Hopefully. I can't believe he was having sex with a chick out in the open." Monie said shaking her head. I wanted to see who she was in case it were Mecca but when he came to speak to me, she stayed put. When she did leave, my back must've been turned because I never got a glimpse of her.

"I'd love to fuck you in a club Monie but never where a man can walk up and see. I'm very selfish of your body." I ran my hands over it as she sat on the hood of the Tesla I purchased her.

It's no secret I have money but so does she. However; as her man, I'm always gonna make sure she's good before anything. That's why she has a brand-new house, truck, my son, a huge ass ring and soon, my last name.

I thought Mecca would've been the woman but Monie booted her right out. It's nothing I wouldn't do for Armonie Banks; include kill.

"Well my cousin has a club we can..." I shushed her with a kiss. I knew about Haven's club and how there were curtains to block people from looking in as well as a sliding door. I haven't been there since me and Monie first hooked up.

"How much do you love me VJ?" I grabbed my phone off the clip and saw Ariel calling me.

"Til infinity baby. Why?" I was about to slide the button to answer.

"I'm pregnant." I lifted my head and she had the biggest smile on her face.

"That's my daughter." I kissed her stomach.

"I hope so." My phone started ringing again.

"What up cuz?"

"Hey. Can you stop by your parents' house?" She asked, which confused me because she knew I was in Virginia.

"When I get back to Jersey." I told her and stared at Monie opening her legs.

"No. I mean the one in Virginia."

"Virginia? You know we put the house up for sale." I was wondering why she even brought their old crib up.

"I know but I'm here and have a surprise for you."

"You're in Virginia?" I asked unsure of why she came.

"Yup. And I haven't something for you."

"A'ight. Can it wait til tomorrow? Monie just gave me some good news and I wanna celebrate." I almost let out a moan when she started sucking on my neck and slipped her hands in my jeans.

"I'm leaving tomorrow. It'll take a minute." She said.

"A'ight. Give me a half hour." I told her and hung up.

"I got you when we get back to the hotel." I lifted her off the truck and helped her in. She was taking her heels off when I hopped in.

"Monie don't you dare." I said when she unzipped my jeans, pulled my dick out and climbed over the seat.

"We haven't had sex in this truck yet."

"Oh fuck!" I had no choice but to pull over. I locked the doors, slid the seat back and pulled her in for a kiss.

"Mmmmm. VJ you feel so good." She moaned and let her head fall back. I slid the straps to her dress down and sucked on her chest.

"Shit Monie." She was grinding in circles wetting my dick up.

"I love you VJ. Oh my gawdddd."

"Show me what I taught you." She nodded, took her knees out the seat and stood on it. Her hands were on my shoulders as she took my ass on one hell of a ride.

"Your ribs ok?" She asked and kissed my neck when we finished.

"Yea. When we get back, I'm definitely gonna need some medication." She laughed and I helped her back in the seat. She grabbed some baby wipes out the glove compartment we kept in there for Legend and cleaned us up.

"Hey." She answered her phone as I pushed my seat up.

"Y'all finished yet?" I heard Brayden through the phone. Both of us looked around.

"Where are you?"

"Man, we rode past y'all twenty minutes ago. Wasn't nobody tryna see what y'all were doing." I started laughing.

"We have to stop by his parents old house."

"I know. Tell VJ to hurry up. He'll appreciate this surprise." I told him ok in the background and drove to my parents' house. I was shocked to see everyone we came with, cars and trucks in the driveway.

"Do you know what Ariel has for me?" I asked Monie.

"Not at all. I didn't even know she was coming here." I grabbed her hand and walked to the door. You could hear people talking and smell the weed stench immediately.

"Well then. Let's see what it is." I opened the door and it got quiet.

Armonie

"Where did you find her?" VJ asked about some woman tied up in a chair. Now that I look, it's the same woman I mentioned having nice shoes at the club. But why is she here and tied up? Her hair was all over the place, makeup running down her face, dress was ripped a little and she only had one shoe on.

"Who is she?" I asked as VJ moved closer and walked around the chair.

"You did all this so I wouldn't find you?" He questioned the woman and yanked her head back.

"Hey boo." Ariel whispered in my ear.

"Hey. Why is everyone quiet and for the last time, who is she?" I asked again with an attitude.

"Mecca." Ariel said and before I could pounce on her Colby Jr held me back. The bitch didn't look anything like I remembered.

"Nah sis. This is his moment."

"You dyed your hair, lost weight and have contacts in. You went through a lot but I still would've recognized you." Mecca started crying. VJ stood in front of her.

"You know why?" She put her head down.

"When you've been with someone as long as we were, you tend to know everything about them. Like the mole you didn't cover on your neck or the gap in your front teeth and the tattoo of my name on your wrist." He flipped her hand over and there it was in bold letters reading VJ.

"You had me down for the count when you stabbed me, but I got up. I told you there wouldn't be anywhere for you to hide." I was a tad bit in my feelings over the fact he remembers certain things about her and hasn't killed her yet.

"I'm sorry VJ. I loved you and you left me for her." She rolled her eyes at me.

"All the years we had in and the plans to raise a family together were flushed down the drain because of her." *Family? Plans?*

"You went to Jersey and forgot about me." VJ lifted her face and stared in a loving way.

"Armonie." Ariel called my name and I saw VJ turn. I walked out the back and noticed Haven sitting out here alone.

"What are you doing here?" I sat on the central air conditioner unit because there weren't any chairs.

"I came to make sure you straight." He passed me the blunt and I told him I couldn't smoke.

"You pregnant again." I nodded my head and wiped my eyes.

"Why you crying?"

"Because he still loves her." He put the blunt out and sat next to me.

"Of course he does." I looked at him

"Armonie they had years in. Did you really think he'd come here and kill her right away?"

"Actually yes. I mean she tried to kill him." He chuckled.

"I'm not excusing what she did but that woman was hurt and felt betrayed. They were fine before he met you then BAM! They're relationship is over, he has a kid with you, moves to be with you and now y'all getting married and having another kid. He didn't do any of that with her. She thought he loved her the same but as you can see, she wasn't where he wanted to be."

"But the way he looked at her and..."

"And you were the same with Freddy in a way." I turned to him

"The nigga was beating on you Armonie and you took that shit so we wouldn't kill him." I sat quiet.

"Regardless of the things he did and could've done, had no one stopped him, he could've killed you and then what?" He made me look at him.

"You still loved Freddy after he hurt you and it's no different with him."

"But what if he regrets killing her and takes her back?" I didn't wanna lose VJ.

"I doubt it. He loves you too much and he'll never allow another man to touch you."

"I wanna believe that but..."

"But nothing. Let that man grieve for her because he will, just like you'll grieve for your ex." He hugged me.

"I'm sorry Armonie." I moved away to look at him.

"I should've never swung off and you wouldn't have gotten hit." He put his head down.

"What's the problem with him?" He leaned back against the wall.

"No one is good enough for you or any of the women in our family. I don't know why you're upset. I did the same thing to Shae fiancé." I laughed because I totally forgot. He actually gave him a harder time then VJ and it's probably because he saw her man more.

"I have to say VJ didn't fold like some of the guys who've tried to date the women in our family. Look at Freddy. Shit, he damn near cried every time we fucked with him. Had you not kept him away, I'm positive he would've cracked." I started laughing.

"Haven, I love you but he's Legend's father and my fiancé." I showed him my ring.

"Damn. Now I have to get Ariel one just as big." He flipped my hand back and forth staring at it.

"You're marrying her?" I smiled.

"Eventually." He shrugged his shoulders.

"You ok?" Ariel stepped out.

"I'm fine." I stood and started walking to the side of the house. I didn't wanna walk out the front door; especially if he's still in there talking to her.

"Where you going?" Ariel asked.

"To sit in my truck. I don't wanna see him struggling to take her life." I shrugged and opened the side gate.

"He didn't Armonie."

"What?"

"When he saw how upset you were, he sliced her throat." I gave her a crazy look.

"Talk to him when y'all get back." Haven said and sat Ariel on his lap. I closed the gate when I walked out and headed to my truck.

I wiped the remaining tears on my face and prepared myself for my man to grieve over a woman who almost killed him. I guess it's the same when it comes to Freddy. I never wanted him to die but he also knew the consequences of my family if he ever did something like that. You don't need a family like mine in order for them to have your back.

I went to open the driver's side door and VJ was sitting in it smoking.

"I'll wait til you're finished."

"I'm done. Get in." He tossed the blunt and unlocked the passenger door. I sat down and felt my neck being pulled closer to him.

"Don't ever get in your feelings around another woman. It'll make her think we're having problems and our union ain't strong. She only said that family shit to hurt you, because I've never discussed any of that with her." He said.

"But the way you stared at her."

"I stared at her that way because I was tryna figure out if I was gonna slice her throat or shoot her."

"I'm sorry. I thought you were going to let her live and…" He smirked.

"I'd never allow her to live and you should know by now, no one is ever gonna take your place." He slipped his tongue in my mouth.

"Are you gonna miss her?" I pulled away.

"Don't stop kissing me to ask no shit like that. Get over here." I took my shoes back off and moved in the seat with him.

"You're about to Mrs. Davis and I think it's time to get used to being married."

"Huh?"

"I want you as my wife by tomorrow morning." He stared at me and I found myself blushing.

"I still make you smile?" He asked.

"Everyday and I'll be your wife tomorrow if that's what you want."

"Let's go." He kissed me and had me sit in my seat.

"Where we going?"

"To the airport."

"The airport?" I questioned

"Las Vegas is a couple hours away. We can be married and still be back before lunchtime." He said and continued driving.

"Are you serious?"

"What? You changed your mind?" He stopped on the side of the road.

"No but our family."

"Our family knows baby." He smiled and drove off without saying another word.

****

"CONGRATULATIONS!" Everyone shouted when we made it back to grams. VJ and I flew to Las Vegas, got married and came right back. When he mentioned our family knowing, I thought he was joking. Yet, here we are with our families all in one place.

"Good job son." Mr. Davis said to VJ and gave both of us a hug.

"Oh my God, you're married now." My mom said and gave me a hug. My dad had to pull her away because she started crying.

"Can y'all excuse us for a minute?" I asked and took VJ in my old room.

"What's wrong?" He asked when we got upstairs.

"Nothing. I wanted to consummate our marriage."

"We did on the plane and before we came over." He smiled and ran his hands up and down my body. When we stepped off the plane, we went home to shower and ended up having more sex.

"I know but I feel like we should consummate here too."

"I don't know Monie, its too many people and shit…" He stopped talking when I kneeled in front of him and devoured his dick.

"You want me to stop?" I asked and stared up at him.

"Noooo. Damn…" He looked down at me smiling and then his head went back, and his eyes started rolling. He guided himself in and out my mouth before emptying all he had.

"I love you Armonie Davis." I smiled when he lifted me in his arms.

"I love you too baby. I'll never hurt you."

"I know you won't because it'll be some murder suicide type shit if you did." I tossed my head back laughing.

103

"You ready for another baby?" I asked him as I grinded on his dick to make him hard again.

"As long as you're my kids' mother, I'm always gonna be ready." He and I stayed in the room for a good hour before joining everyone at the party.

"How y'all fucking and we down here celebrating the marriage?" Colby Jr. asked and mushed me in the head.

"Where you going?" I asked because he was walking to the door.

"Let me talk to you for a minute." VJ kissed my lips and went to where his family was. I glanced around and noticed Ariel sitting on Haven's lap and he was smiling. Hopefully, things will stay the same.

"You remember Will Sanchez?" He asked.

"He graduated high school with me. Why?" He sat down on the step.

"Jacinta cheated on me with him."

"Wait a minute. Doesn't he work for you? Like didn't you put him on and he was making good money, because his sister told me he purchased her a brand new truck not too long

104

ago." I sat next to him and had to move slow. VJ and I were having so much sex, my pussy was super sore.

"He busting that ass open." Colby said and I pushed him on the arm.

"I'm happy for you sis. You deserve to be happy."

"I'm very happy and thanks for not treating him like shit." I looked and he was playing with Legend.

"Haven will come around Monie. It may take some time, but he will."

"You think so? I mean they don't have to be friends. I'm just tired of missing our Sunday dinners."

"So does he."

"How you find out about Jacinta?" I asked to get back to what we were discussing.

"Ciara told me." I started laughing.

"What?"

"You sleeping with her though. She may be telling you anything." Ciara was one of the many women my brother slept with. I think she loved him but he only had feelings for Jacinta.

"I thought the same until she went out with her sister to some restaurant up north, and sent me actual video of Jacinta and Will kissing and feeling all over each other. She even followed them to some hotel, and it showed them going in doing the same. It don't take a scientist to know they fucked."

"Aren't you cheating on her?" I gave him the side eye.

"You know I could forgive her if it weren't someone close. This nigga knew she was my girl like everyone else. Regardless, if he felt bad for Jacinta or not, it wasn't up to him to fuck her." I didn't say anything because he's right. You never sleep with your friend's girl. He didn't even address the fact he's doing the same thing.

"What you gonna do?"

"He's gotta go and as far as her, I don't know yet." He leaned back on the steps.

"Well if you need me to whoop her ass, I'll be ready."

"No more fighting for you. Those days are over." VJ walked over saying.

"You good?" VJ asked Colby. They were cordial and actually got along really well.

"Yea. I had to talk to sis for a minute." Colby Jr. kissed me on the cheek and went to join everyone in the other rooms.

"No more fighting Monie." VJ sat next to me on the step.

"I have to beat up Latifa for tryna kill me."

"She'll be handled soon. Promise me no more fighting."

"VJ." I whined.

"Armonie Davis." I shut right up. I loved hearing him call me by his last name.

"Fine."

"Good. Come with me to eat. Grams cooked a bunch of food and my daughter needs to eat." He rubbed my stomach and carried me in the kitchen bridal style.

"Didn't you carry her over the threshold already?" Brayden asked.

"Yup and later I'm gonna carry her all over my…"

"VJ." I shouted and he stopped. Brayden told him he play too much.

The rest of the night seem to be going perfect until I saw Haven walking outside. VJ was already out there smoking with Brayden, Jax and Colby Jr. My dad and uncles were out there too but I didn't feel like leaving right now.

Haven

"If you say one word to him, I swear we're not having anymore sex." Ariel spoke quietly in my ear. I saw my pops and other family members going out to smoke and decided to do the same. I saw VJ when he went out, but I told Monie and everyone else I'd keep my mouth shut.

"Be quiet and stop threatening me with sex. As you say, your sexual appetite is the same as mine; therefore, you'll want the dick." She rolled her eyes.

"What up?" I stepped outside and Brayden's father walked over to me as I sat at the table rolling a blunt.

"A cheater and a baby." He said and I busted out laughing.

"Yo, I should tell her you blackmailing me."

"I forgot to add snitch to your resume." He sipped his beer and introduced me to some other guys who he did business with. I spoke and continued rolling up.

"Hey brother." Christian sat next to me.

"Where the hell you been?" I asked and pulled the lighter out my pocket.

"Stressing." He responded and I looked at him.

"Stressing for what? The divorce went through, and you should be living your best life."

"I should with Stormy but she doesn't wanna speak to me." He sounded sad as hell.

"Why not?"

"I told you she claims to have some secret she held in all this time and scared to tell me." I shook my head.

"Well you know ain't none of us ever fucked her so that ain't it." He laughed.

"I don't think she can have kids." I stopped smoking and looked at him.

"Did she tell you that?"

"No but Haven the first time we had sex, I didn't wear a condom and there was no way, I'd wear one after being inside."

"I feel you on that." I told him because once you felt the inside of a woman without a condom and she feels good, it's no way you strapping up.

"Anyway, she's not pregnant and it's the only thing I can think of."

"Ariel didn't get pregnant right away." I mentioned to him not too long ago how it took her a while. She finally told me it was due to the depo shot.

"But she's pregnant now and Stormy's not."

"Let me ask you this." I took a pull and blew the smoke in the other direction. I'm disrespectful but I know my brother is into church big time so I wouldn't do that.

"Do you want more kids?" I asked because he didn't have anymore after CJ.

"Well yea."

"What if she can't have kids? Are you gonna stop messing with her?"

"They're other ways to have kids." He responded.

"Did you tell her?"

"No because she's still hasn't told me that's what it is."
He shrugged.

"Women." I shook my head and finished speaking to
my brother.

"Uncle Haven. I want some money." My nephew CJ
said walking over to me with his hand out. I loved my nephew
and was happy as hell his mother was no longer my sister in
law.

"CJ, you know better." Christian yelled.

"Fine. I'll just shoot you then." He pulled out this fake
gun and aimed it at me.

"Yo! What the fuck?" Everyone got quiet when
Christian cursed. He slipped up on occasions but not in front of
his son.

"Where did you hear that at?" Christian asked.

"Mommy says she wishes uncle Haven died and when I
get older to kill him." I nodded and looked around to see
everyone staring at me.

"Tell that..." I started to say.

"DON'T YOU DARE HAVEN!" My mother shouted and walked over to CJ. I didn't even know she was out here. My mom barely ever gets mad but her facial expression said it all.

"Go inside CJ." She told him.

"I'm sorry grandma." He turned to me.

"I would never kill you uncle Haven. I love you." He ran over and hugged me before running in the house.

"Christian, I am not a fighter but either you or Haven better find that bitch and get rid of her." She started crying.

"Passion." My pops walked behind her.

"No Wolf. I've sat around watching her treat both of my sons like shit and trying to stay out of it, I did nothing because she was married to Christian and had my grandson. I will not sit around and let her wish for CJ to kill his uncle. She has to be taken care of or I swear to God, I'll go to jail for killing her myself." She stormed off in the house and I think all of us were stunned because it was quiet as hell.

"HAVEN WHAT DID YOU DO?" My cousin Monie came out the door yelling with Ariel and my aunts behind her.

"Not right now Monie." VJ pulled her away and I understood why.

"What happened Haven? Are you ok?" Ariel asked and for the first time, I let a tear drop in front of my entire family.

My mother has gotten mad over the years about a lotta things and yes, she cried but tonight it was different. She was actually contemplating a murder just to make sure her kids and grandson were safe. My mother is very shy, passionate, outgoing and will do any and everything for anyone. To see her like that hurt me to my soul and Elaina has to be dealt with.

When Christian mentioned her going to the cops and possibly the feds, I wasn't worried because of the connections I had. Yea, she filed a report but as fast as she did it, is as fast as it got tossed. Then she approached Stormy and her mother in the store, pissing my brother off and I still let her live because he really wanted CJ to grow up with her but I couldn't stall her out any longer. She had to go, and she had to go now.

I stood up to leave and noticed Brayden stand with me. He stopped fucking with me for a minute and I thought nothing of it because VJ is his cousin. However; when it's time for the reaper to show his face, he's never turned his back on me. I nodded and asked him to give me a minute. I needed to check on my mom and make sure she's alright.

"Hey nephew. Can I talk to nana for a minute?" CJ was sitting on her lap wiping her tears.

"I'm sorry uncle Haven. Can you make nana happy again?" He kissed her cheek, hugged me and ran out the room. I closed the door and sat next to her.

"I have never wanted a person removed from the earth more than her. Even Christian's father didn't make me wish death on him like this woman does."

"I'm gonna handle it."

"Haven." I stared at my mother and wiped her tears. She's beautiful to me and has a heart of gold. It's why my father fell in love with her.

"You are your fathers' child, so I know you'll handle it. What I don't want is to visit my child in jail either."

"I'll be ok ma."

"That's just it Haven. You always say that, but I want you to be better than ok. I want you living your life to the fullest with no regrets. You possibly going to jail will be the biggest regret I'll have if by some chance you get caught. I know I'm upset but just forget it. Karma will get her." I kissed my mom on the cheek and stood when the door opened. My pops walked in with Christian, Shae and my other siblings.

"I'll make it look like an accident so when CJ gets older and search how she died; it won't be from murder.

"Haven please." She cried.

"He's gonna be fine Passion." My father said and sat behind her on the bed.

"I'm coming." Christian said and kissed my mom on the cheek.

"Both of y'all be careful." She blew us a kiss and cried in my father's arms. Oh, I'm gonna make that bitch Elaina suffer alright.

"I'm out." I told Brayden who was speaking to his cousin.

"Hey everyone." We all looked to the door and it was Stormy. I told Christian to handle his business with her and I'll let him know about Elaina when it's done. I know he loved

Stormy and wanted to tackle whatever issue she had so I wasn't even mad.

"Haven are you gonna be ok?" Ariel asked and I pulled her in one of the rooms.

"I'm gonna be fine. Are you gonna wait for me here or at the house?"

"If you're not here and it gets late, I'll see you at home." I smiled because she asked me to move in with her a few days ago.

"I'll see you at home then." I pulled her in for a kiss and rubbed her stomach.

"Have Grams put some food in Tupperware for me." She nodded.

"Text me as soon as you get to the house too. I may not text back, but I'll see it."

"Ok. Haven be careful." I kissed her again and opened the door.

"Always."

I stepped out the room, out the house and went to my car. Colby Jr. hopped in with me and Jax hopped in with

Brayden. I had no idea where we were going or where this bitch was but I'm definitely gonna finish her tonight.

Christian

"Umm. Is everything ok? Should I come back another time?" Stormy asked because everyone had a sad look on their face.

"No it's ok. Hey Stormy." Armonie walked over and gave her a hug.

"Congratulations. You're married now." She gushed over the ring VJ gave her and I stayed in the corner until she finished.

"I know right. I'm hoping Ariel and you are next. I mean Shae getting married next month and Colby Jr was supposed to marry Jacinta, but everything isn't playing out the way I thought."

"As long as you're happy you can't worry about anyone else."

"I want everyone to be happy like me." Armonie was ecstatic to be married and a mommy. I don't ever recall her being this happy with Freddy and after learning he was beating on her, I see why.

"Hey Stormy." VJ spoke and asked Armonie where Legend's bag was. Grams had him and he needed to be changed.

"Let me go find it. I'll talk to you in a few." Armonie stepped off and I grabbed Stormy's hand, asked my sister Shae to tell my mom I'll be back and that CJ was staying with grams. She gave Stormy a hug and I exited the house with her. I could feel her resistance as I held her hand but I didn't let go until we were at the car.

"We can speak out here or at my house." I told her.

"Your house?" I hadn't seen her to let her know I purchased a new place from Ariel's dad.

When he started building, Armonie told me I should look into it. I did and now we're two streets over from one another. Ariel's father was doing the damn thing when it came to real estate and now that VJ's here, he'll be the one running it with Brayden. Well, we know what Brayden will be doing with my brother but it's a cover up for sure.

"Get in." She hesitated at first but eventually sat in the car. I didn't say two words to her on the way over and once we got to my house, I left her in the car. I'm not about to baby her. I did pick my phone up and dial Haven.

"Yo!" Haven answered on the second ring.

"I don't care what time you get done. Call and let me know you're alright."

"You supposed to be fucking some sense into Stormy. How you calling me?" I laughed.

"I love you bro and be careful."

"I love you too and I will." He hung up and I heard the door close.

"Sit." I pointed to the couch.

"Christian."

"Not right now Stormy." I stripped out my clothes and called her to me.

"I'm not here for this." She bit down on her lip.

"I think you are." I walked over to her and watched as she stroked my dick gently.

"You're gonna tell me everything as soon as I finish fucking your brains out."

"Mmmm. Shit Christian." She took my dick out her mouth and looked at me.

"I love that you're a deacon but when you bring that hood out, it turns me on even more." She went back to sucking and I stopped her.

"Good because I'm not making love to you tonight." I yanked her up by the hair and aggressively kissed her. I literally tore her clothes off, ripped her panties off and rammed myself inside.

"Fuckkkkkk!" She cried out and dug her nails deep in my back.

"I'm about to cum Stormy because it's been a minute but you're gonna suck me off until I get hard again and then it's on." I felt my nut coming up and released myself inside her. Like the nasty freak she is, she did what I said and soon after, I had her bent over the couch fucking her in both holes.

"Christian, I can't. Oh my gawdddd. I'm cumming again." I felt her juices leaking and dug deeper and went harder.

"Whatever you're hiding from me, I want you to tell me. You hear me?" She bit down on the pillow and started screaming.

"You heard me?"

"Yes. Christian, I love you so much. Promise you won't leave when I tell you." I wrapped my hand around her throat, pulled out her pussy and pushed my dick back in her ass.

"I'm not going nowhere, and we'll get through whatever it is. Shit." Her ass was so tight I could feel my nut building.

"I love you Stormy. Don't leave me again." I went faster.

"I won't. Oh gawdddd. I won'tttttt..." She shouted and I let go.

"Damn. I gotta get mad and fuck you like this more often." I laid on the floor and she fell on top of me. We were both breathing fast.

"I can't have kids." I ran my hand down her back.

"I know."

123

"Who told you?" She sat up and I could feel both of our juices falling out of her.

"I figured it out."

"How?" She questioned.

"You hadn't gotten pregnant and I know you weren't taking any pills or had abortions. What else could it be?"

"I have endometriosis." I sat on my elbows to look at her.

"A lotta women have that and still reproduce."

"Yes but a few years ago, I went to see a doctor about preserving my eggs." She seemed embarrassed.

"Why?"

"It was a precaution. Anyway, I went through the procedure and he said I had tons of eggs but the only problem is my body couldn't carry them."

"Ok."

"I had him take as many as he could in case I got married and wanted to have children in the future." I nodded because this is another scenario women went through.

"I went to see a doctor in New York. He was a specialist and after talking to him I realized the best thing for me was to get a hysterectomy. It would alleviate the pain, but I'd never be able to birth my own kids."

"Is that why you disappeared a few years ago?"

"Yes. I had the surgery, stayed in the hospital for three weeks due to complications and when I came home my mom took care of me.

"Why didn't you tell me?"

"I know you want more kids and..." I shushed her with my index finger.

"And we can adopt or use your eggs and my sperm in a surrogate."

"You'd do that?"

"Stormy we've been friends a lot longer than lovers and even if you were with someone else and decided to let someone be your surrogate, I'd still be by your side." She started crying.

"Is that the only thing you were hiding?"

"That and your ex-wife constantly accusing me of sleeping around." I laughed.

"Yea. Evidently you broke us up and you're a whore, blah, blah, blah." I laughed after saying it. My ex-wife was in denial like crazy.

"I never slept with anyone after we've been intimate." She reminded me.

"I believe you and same here."

"I'm sorry for disappearing Christian. I didn't know how to tell you."

"Don't do it again or I'm gonna make that pussy even more sore."

"It's worth it." She smiled and the two of us ended up fucking each other's brains out before stopping to shower and get something to eat.

****

DING! DONG! I heard the doorbell and asked Stormy to get it. Haven was on his way to tell me what happened with Elaina's mom. He couldn't find my ex and did something to her mother instead.

"I told you to stay away from him."

"Elaina?" I said out loud to myself and ran in the other room.

"Calm down Elaina." Stormy had her hands in the air backing up.

"What are you doing?" I went to block Stormy and wasn't quick enough.

BOOM! Elaina shot her in the stomach.

"Oh shit." I caught Stormy before she fell, and gently laid her on the ground. I had no idea what to do and started panicking myself.

"Tha fuck happened?" Haven yelled. Him, Colby Jr, Brayden and Jax ran in.

"I had her answer the door because I thought it was you and Elaina... Elaina... shot her..." It's like my body was shutting down watching Stormy cry and beg me not to let her die.

"The ambulance is gonna take too long." Haven said and they lifted her up.

"Change your clothes." Brayden said and I sat there.

"GET UP CHRISTIAN. YOU HAVE TO CHANGE BEFORE GOING DOWN THERE."

"Where are they taking her?"

"To the hospital. Let's go." He helped me off the floor and I heard him on the phone telling someone to hurry up and get there to clean the mess.

I took a quick shower to wash Stormy's blood off, threw on some clothes and rushed down stairs. By the time I reached the bottom step, two guys were walking in with stuff in their hands. Brayden told them they better be finished in the next two minutes and I'll be damned if they weren't. The blood was off the floor and they used some light to check for remnants. When they saw nothing, I locked up and walked out with Brayden.

"Is she gonna be ok?"

"She'll be fine Christian. What happened?" We got in my truck and I began explaining how Elaina told her to leave me alone and shot her.

"From here on out. Elaina will never be a problem." He spoke with confidence. Did he know something I didn't?

"But..."

"All you need to concern yourself with is making sure your girl is good." I nodded and called her parents.

"Hey Christian." Her father answered. It sounded like he was in a car.

"Umm. Mr. Burns. I don't know how to tell you this but..."

"I already know. They've taken her into surgery. I'm in route to the hospital." He cut me off.

"Huh? How did you know?" He chuckled a little.

"When you're a pastor and your daughter is dating the deacon, everyone knows. And in knowing that, they know who Stormy is."

"Oh." I wasn't sure what he said made sense but I'm sure it did to him.

"When Haven and your cousin brought her in the hospital, the doctor on call is one of my college buddies. He had them contact me so he could work on my daughter." I couldn't believe he knew everything that fast.

"I'm sorry pastor. I had no idea Elaina knew where I lived." She had to have followed me because my new address isn't even on the documents at the courthouse.

"She's gonna be ok Christian. I'm leaving it in God's hands and he's never let me down."

"I'll be right there."

"Ok." He hung up and a ten minutes later Brayden pulled up to the ER.

"Christian. Are you ok?" Her mom ran over to check me. I thought she'd be upset or cursing me out.

"I'm fine. Did they say how long?"

"No. Have they found Elaina?" Brayden looked over at my brother who nodded.

"That's all I needed to see." The pastor said and took a seat with his wife.

"She's going to be fine Christian." Her mom patted my shoulder.

"I hope so." I leaned my head against the wall and waited with everyone else.

Stormy

"You're not gonna die Stormy." I heard Christian crying but my body was in so much pain, I couldn't respond after asking him not to let me.

When Elaina pointed the gun at me, it was no doubt in my mind that she wasn't going to use it. She considered me to be the woman in her way. The woman who kept Christian from trying to make things work with her. And the woman she knew would raise her son after Haven killed her.

What I couldn't understand and still don't is why isn't she taking responsibility for her actions? She's the one who caused all this drama in her relationship; not me. If she wanted it to work between her and Christian, she should've tried harder. Instead she blamed the woman who had nothing to do with it. Now I'm lying here in the hospital bed watching the lights flash on the ceiling because I couldn't move.

My body was weak and I had no idea where the nurses button was, or the one to raise the bed so I could at least see if anyone is in the room. My mouth had something in it; therefore,

I couldn't speak. I did however; move each one of my body parts to see if I were paralyzed. Thankfully, I was able to move each one, but it didn't explain why I had wires coming down my head.

"Welcome back Miss Burns." I heard someone say and then a light flashed in my eyes. It was the tiny flashlight doctors kept in their pockets.

"Nurse. Let her parents know she's awake but tell them to give me ten minutes to do an exam before coming in." The nurse responded and I laid there as the doctor slowly removed the tube out my mouth, one out my pussy and the monitors off my head.

He ran a metal object down my legs and feet to check for movement. Once he finished, a nurse stepped in with my mom and sister who both cried and hugged me tight. My sister had to pull my mother off because she wouldn't let go.

"I'm ok mom but you're hurting me."

"I'm sorry. We're gonna get you in the shower." The doctor and a male tech lifted me in a chair and then into the shower chair. They stepped out and her and my sister washed me up. I couldn't take a real shower due to the bandage on my stomach, but they washed me up and I no longer smelled like the hospital.

"Where's daddy?" I asked looking around.

"Outside."

"How long have I been here?"

"A week and a half." My mother answered.

"No way." I couldn't believe it.

"You lost so much blood they had to put you in a coma. We've been waiting for you to wake up." I felt like VJ did when he told Monie he only felt like he was asleep for a day.

"Is Christian ok? Did she shoot him?" I was worried she got him too.

"He's fine and I see you told him." My mom smiled as my sister brushed my hair.

"How do you know?"

"Let's just say, he did what he had to at the doctor's office here, and the next step is for y'all to pick a surrogate." I couldn't stop the tears if I wanted to.

"He loves you sis and if you can't find a suitable surrogate, I'll do it for you." My sister Bianca said.

"I would never ask you." My sister is a lesbian, full blown. She's a femme and has never been with a man.

"Sis, one day me and Fay are gonna want to have kids and you and I both know she's not carrying the baby." We all shared a laugh.

"But what if you get attached to the baby and..." That's my main concern, even with a surrogate.

What if the person becomes heavily attached to the baby in their stomach? I couldn't deal with that pain too.

"And I'd never do that to you. I love you Stormy and I know it's been hard living with this. Let me help you." She sat next to me and wiped the tears.

"Don't look at me. Fay told her if she didn't offer, she'd look at her different."

"Fay ain't going nowhere." My sister said and I had to agree. Fay is very butch and from the outside looking in, you wouldn't know she's a chick. However; she's the same way

134

over my sister as I've seen most men over their women. She didn't play any games when it came to her.

"I have to see what Christian says." I told them.

"He wants whatever you want." I started crying again when my dad walked in.

"You ok sis?" My brother Hassan strolled in with his new wife. I loved them together and they're expecting their second child.

"I'm ok. Where's my niece?"

"Your grandmother said she couldn't come." He pointed to my mother.

"Ma."

"Be quiet. My grand baby ain't got no business in this hospital. You can see her at home." My mother was very protective of my niece and my father, she could do no wrong in his eyes. Ever since Christian and I been together, they've claimed CJ as their grandchild too.

"It's about time you came back to me." Christian stepped in with balloons and flowers

"Who told you I woke up?" He sat them on the table.

135

"Your father called when I went home to change."

"You stayed up here?" I asked unsure of why.

"I only left because your parents said I needed to change. After the first two days they said I was starting to stink."

"Awww baby. You never left my side."

"Not until they made me." He moved passed them and pecked my lips. I was so in love with this man. What was I thinking keeping a secret from him?

****

"Are you sure Bianca?" I asked my sister ten times if she were sure about doing this surrogate thing.

"Don't ask me again. Christian get your girl." We were at the doctor's office in New York getting ready to have my sister inseminated. I don't know how they made it possible as quick as they did but here we are. I've only been out the hospital a week and I fought with all of them to come here.

My whole family came, and Christian's mom and his aunt Journey did as well. Venus wanted to come but she said the manager at one of her shops called out, so she had to fill in.

Armonie and Ariel tried to but neither one of their men allowed it, being they're already pregnant. They said the ride was too long and my brother showed up ten minutes ago. I couldn't believe the amount of support we both had.

"Relax Stormy." He held my hand. Fay was looking over the paperwork with Bianca.

"She's gonna be fine." Christian's mom said and held my hand.

"Ok. I'm just worried."

"I'm gonna make you wait in the car." My mother said and collected the jewelry my sister wore.

"Ok and thank you Fay for allowing her to do this." She came and kneeled in front of me.

"Your sister is going to be my wife one day and we'll get to experience this for ourselves. She's doing this because you're her sister and family stick together. We love you Stormy and all of us are praying it happens on this first try. If not, we'll keep trying until it does." She kissed my cheek and sat back next to my sister.

"I'm nervous."

137

"She's not having surgery Stormy. Relax." My father said and had all of us bow our heads to pray. Of course he's not ok with the lifestyle my sister chose but he loves Fay just the same. After the prayer, we sat there waiting.

"Bianca Burns." The nurse called out. My sister kissed my parents, then my cheek and Fay.

"Keep your fingers crossed I come out pregnant." Soon as the doors closed my father definitely said another prayer. I hope it works.

Haven

"You sure about this?" I asked my brother as we pulled up to Armonie's hotel.

"Yup. You saw ma's face just like I did. Ain't no way Elaina can stay around." He said with finality.

"What about CJ? I was gonna make it look like an accident, but I thought torture was much better." I smirked

The night Elaina shot Stormy, we were already pulling in the driveway, as she pulled out. I looked straight in her face and she flipped me the finger. I couldn't leave because at the time we didn't know what happened and I had to check on my brother.

I sent my cousin Jax after her in Brayden's truck since we were altogether. He didn't wanna cause a scene and waited until she pulled into some run-down motel. She must've been staying there.

Anyway, he watched her go inside, knocked on the door and yanked her dumb ass out. Who answers the door right after you commit a crime? She did the normal kicking, screaming and begging him not to take her. Jax said she even offered sex, in which he punched her in the face at that point. We're no woman beaters but if we're about to kill you, your gender doesn't matter.

"He'll be ok. I just wanna be able to tell ma it's done and she's no longer a concern." I nodded and tossed the last of my blunt on the ground.

"What y'all doing here?" Armonie was standing at the desk with the manager.

"You nosy." Christian said.

"Ugh yea. I'll be right back." She told the chick and walked up to us.

"Monie, I thought you were coming in for papers. What you doing?" We all turned and saw VJ coming in our direction.

"I am but they came and..."

"And if both of them are here with no women, I think you know what it is. Let's go." He put his hand on the small of her back and started leading her away.

"VJ, I am a grown woman and...

140

"And if you don't come on and let them handle business, guess who not sleeping with your spoiled ass tonight?" She looked at him, then us, then back to him.

"Ughhhh. Whatever." She stormed off and went back to the lady.

"That's what yo ass gets. Bye cuz." She told me to fuck off and I saw VJ waiting for her by the desk.

"He really does love her." Christian said and pressed the elevator button.

"I'd hope so. They married with a son and another on the way." We stepped on and pressed the B button for basement.

"I'm happy she got away from Freddy. Matter of fact, where his sister?" He asked and the bitch went into hiding. I'm not as concerned with her at this moment because VJ isn't gonna allow anyone to get her.

"I have people searching for her now." He shook his head

"A'ight bro. This is it. It's now or never." He ran his hand down his face. I had no doubt it would be hard for him but he knew like I did, it had to be done. I opened the door and he shook his head.

"Pastor Burns." Yup the pastor was in here with his wife talking to Brayden and Colby Jr.

"It's about time." He said and Christian looked at me.

"Oh, you thought we wouldn't have a say in this woman dying?" He pointed to Elaina.

"But…"

"I am the pastor, but I haven't always been." He winked.

"I think it's only fair we observe or partake in her demise. After all, she did try and murder my daughter. What you think Serena?"

"I told Haven to kill her the same day he mentioned finding her." She shrugged and I laughed.

"Why does she have that on her?" He pointed to the black elastic holding her eyelids up and the tongs I used to keep someone's mouth open. I walked over to Elaina's mother who lost her bowels five times already.

"Well. I thought it would be a great idea for Elaina to witness her mother take her last breath. We didn't want her to close them." I nodded to Brayden who already had his gloves on. He pulled the goggles down and started the chainsaw. This time Elaina's mom passed out. Elaina shook her head over and over.

"I told you various times to respect royalty and you couldn't listen. Then, you went to the feds to get me locked up. Oh, Christian I forgot to mention she's the reason the cops began investigating me."

"WHAT?"

"Yea. Evidently, your ex-wife went to them months before the divorce claiming I'm a murderer and she was scared for her life. They tried building a case and even had statements from Elaina. I couldn't believe after all the chances I gave her to stay alive, she went behind my back." I shook my head.

"Yooooo! That's crazy." Colby said about Brayden cutting Elaina's mom leg off.

"Why Elaina?"

"Sorry bro but she screams too much. I'm not taking it off." Colby said about the duct tape he just put on her mouth.

"I'm doing the head." Colby shouted and put gloves and goggles on. Now it was Elaina's turn to lose her bowels.

BANG! BANG! I rolled my eyes because it only meant Armonie was at the door.

"What?" I opened it.

"I have a right to see." She folded her arms.

"Where's your husband?" I looked around because it's no way in hell, he knows she's down here.

"He went to the room for something. Hurry up." She pushed me out the way and soon as she took a few steps, her body was being lifted right out.

"Armonie, I have a major problem with this." VJ had her against the wall outside the door.

"How did you know where I was?"

"Not the point. Why are you down here?" He towered over her waiting for an answer.

"I wanted to see..."

"Why? Huh? You don't need to see everything Armonie." He spoke firmly to her without yelling.

"I know but..."

"But nothing. I'm not feeling this and if you can't listen, then married or not we need to take a break."

"What? So, if you can't control me like my ex you don't wanna be with me? Is that what you've become?" She tried to turn this on him.

"If I can't control you? Is that why you think I don't want you down here?" He shook his head.

"What else is it? I'm not doing what you say so let's take a break?" He scoffed up a laugh.

"If you think I wanna control you, then maybe you weren't ready to be married. I'm out." He brushed past her, and me, Colby, Brayden and Christian all stared at her.

"WHAT?" She barked at us.

"I may not fuck with him Monie but he's right and you were dead ass wrong." I left her standing there and asked Christian to stay out there with her. He may want his ex-dead, but he doesn't wanna see it.

145

"I apologize for the interruption, but my cousin has a hard time listening." Pastor Burns started laughing.

"Anyway, let's get this done." I handed the knife to Stormy's mother and watched her rip the duct tape off and slice Elaina's tongue out.

"That's for cursing in the church and talking shit to my daughter." I was about to say something when Mrs. Burns went on a stabbing spree. I mean she was fucking Elaina up. Pastor Burns was shaking his head.

"I think she dead." Brayden said and we started laughing.

"Colby can you cut her head off too?" Mrs. Burns asked. His crazy ass started the Chainsaw back up and Elaina's head rolled on the ground.

"Perfect. Now I can sleep knowing she's gone for good. You ready?" Mrs. Burns unzipped the jumper she had on that had blood splattered all over it and asked where the incinerator was.

"Let me find out you planned this." She smiled and walked out.

"Have this cleaned up in two minutes." We watched as the bodies, limbs and heads were tossed down the incinerator and the hoses turned on to flush the blood down the drain. Brayden and Colby cleaned themselves up and I did the same. Two minutes went by fast and as usual; it looks as if nothing happened.

"Thanks Haven. I appreciate it." Both of her parents hugged me.

"Of course. I think we all know Stormy is about to be our sister in law."

"She better. Especially if they have kids." Her mom said. She is a piece of work.

"My moms been praying every night for it to happen." I wasn't lying. She wanted Christian and Stormy together too and wanted them to have kids. She may not birth the child physically, but it's his sperm and her egg so it's their child. Even if they decide to adopt, that's still my niece or nephew.

"Me too. And make sure you bring your baby by to get Christened at church. We don't need him or her growing up like you."

"Hey, I was christened there."

"I don't think I put enough holy water on you." The pastor said and we all busted out laughing. I left with them and noticed Monie sitting on the couch crying. I blew my breath and took a seat next to her.

"What's wrong?" I asked.

"He don't love me no more."

"Why you say that?" I leaned back in the seat.

"Because he left me and won't answer his phone."

"Armonie y'all married. He ain't going nowhere and stop being dramatic."

"I just don't want anyone controlling me." She wiped her eyes.

"He wasn't tryna control you. You need to talk to your husband."

"Am I doing something wrong?" She looked at me.

"I can't answer that but today you had no business coming down there. I'm not sure how he knows about that area, but you don't need to be privy to everything." She went to speak, and I held my hand up.

148

"It doesn't matter if it's your hotel. You know what we do and because you acted like a brat, you made him leave. Take it from me Armonie. You're gonna push him away." I stood up.

"I don't want to. I just thought…"

"He's not Freddy." She shook her head and asked for a ride home.

I dropped her off and VJ's car wasn't there. I waited for her to go in and pulled off. I knew he had security out the ass, so no one was in there. I pulled up in the driveway of the house Ariel made me move into, took my ass in to shower and passed out next to my girl.

Ariel

"Armonie you were wrong." I told her when I stopped by the house this morning.

Haven came in late last night and fell straight to sleep. When he woke up and told me what she did I was mad. How can she even assume VJ was tryna control her is beyond me? Then she made it like him and Freddy were the same, which is a smack in the face if you ask me. Now she's sitting here crying her eyes out because VJ didn't come home.

My aunt called me up to ask why he stayed over there. I gave her a short version, but she said, Monie had to grow up and we all know VJ ain't going nowhere. He's not but it definitely made her realize who he is.

"I just wanted to see what they were doing." She whined.

"And then what? You would've seen it and then possibly had nightmares. You're pregnant just like me and even though I witnessed them torture Elaina and her mom, I'd never want to see anyone die." She didn't say anything. I've

150

seen people die at the hospital, but it was nothing like how Haven and them did it.

"How did VJ know about the room?" I asked because none of us told him. Even if Brayden did, he probably didn't know where it was.

"I took him down there before."

"Why?"

"I was showing him the place and he knows about the family." She shrugged her shoulders.

"What did he say?" She rolled her eyes.

"What did he say Armonie?" I asked again.

"I should never go down there because it's not a place for a woman."

"Ok. Did you have a problem when he said it?"

"No but no one was there."

"How can you be ok with him telling you he didn't want you down there and then get mad when he asks you why you were there?" Again, she said nothing.

"Well, I have to meet my dad at the new building. You wanna come?" I asked to get her out the house.

"Yea. Let me get Legend ready." She went upstairs and I sent Haven a message telling him to pick milk up on the way home. I hated going into the 7/11's for milk and I wasn't going on the grocery store.

VJ

"Can I get another shot of Hennessy?" I asked the bartender and turned around to see some chick fucking the pole up. I mean she was doing the damn thing.

I was at the club because Monie pissed me off yesterday doing that dumb shit. I didn't go out last night and since Brayden home with his chick, I decided to come out for a drink. It's been a minute and I deserve one.

"Here you go." She passed it to me and I tossed it back.

"Hey sexy." I looked to my right and this woman was pretty too.

"What up?" I requested a beer from the bartender.

"You not from here?" I lifted my drink and sipped as this chick let her eyes roam my body more than once. I felt like a bitch and a nigga was hitting on me.

"Why you ask that?"

"Your accent is different. Very southern like." She said and followed me to the front. I was feeling tipsy and needed a seat but not at the bar. I wasn't drunk and knew everything going on but I still wanted to drink in peace.

"Yo! Are all the VIP's taken?" The woman searched the paper. For some reason this other chick was still behind me.

"There's one left. It's $1500 and you get two bottles."

"$1500. Damn. Alright." I handed her my card and watched her stare at it.

"What? My shit work."

"It's not that. Umm, let me take you to VIP and I'll get your fee from up there." The woman stood and I followed her up the steps and noticed the chick right behind me. I didn't say a word.

"This one is for you." She pressed a button and the sliding doors opened.

"I can see why this one is expensive." There were two televisions on the wall, a loveseat, a mini bar and two buckets of bottles. In any case, this spot is nice as fuck. I noticed the red panic button too.

"Thanks."

"Is she with you?" I turned and the same woman was standing there.

"Yes. Didn't you see me walk up here with him?" I shook my head and poured myself a drink.

"Ok. I'll be back for your card." The lady left but the other woman remained.

"I didn't think she'd ever leave." This bitch started taking her clothes off.

"YO! Tha fuck are you doing?" I felt like pressing the panic button myself. I don't need my wife's family coming in here and she naked.

"I'm married and not interested. Whatever you thought was gonna happen; ain't." She walked up on me and tried to grab my dick.

"I will break your fucking wrist in here if you don't get dressed and bounced."

"You're hurting me." Tears were leaving her eyes.

"You were right about me not being from here because where I'm from, I don't play this shit." I pushed her so hard, she almost fell over the banister outside the VIP.

"What the..." She came towards me in a fighting stance and outta nowhere, my wife grabbed the back of her hair and dragged her down the steps. *Who told her where I was?* I sat my ass right on the couch, put my feet up and finished drinking.

A few minutes later Monie strolled in, pressed the sliding door and made the curtains closed.

"At least give me competition." She said and took a seat on the small table in front of me.

"I told you before Monie; no one will ever compare to you. You're one of a kind baby." She blushed.

"I think my husband is one of a kind and I should've listened when he spoke to me." She opened her legs and revealed her naked pussy in that short skirt.

"Keep going." Her index finger was in her mouth as she slid her foot on my dick.

"I know you're not him or trying to control me. I'm sorry." I sipped my drink.

"How sorry?"

"Let me show you." Monie stood and removed all her clothes. She turned around and stood there. I sat up, put my

156

drink down and slid my finger across the tattoo above her ass, where people consider it to be the tramp stamp spot.

"How the fuck did they give you a tattoo and you pregnant?" She smirked. Her stomach wasn't showing so I guess its how she got away with it.

"I didn't tell them and it's the only way I could make it up to you."

"Monie." I loved how she wanted to make it up to me, but this is too much.

"Don't be mad. I'll go to the doctors tomorrow and make sure everything's ok."

"Hell yea you are. Why didn't you put VJ?" The shit was nice as hell.

"Because it's not your real name and your ex had VJ on her." I started laughing,

"Do you like it?" She turned to look at me over her shoulder.

"I love it. Bend over." I let my hand guide her body down, spread her legs and licked my lips at how pretty her pussy was. Her juices were leaking out and I couldn't wait to taste her.

"Sssss." Her hands were on the table as I dove right in. In the process of me eating her pussy, I unbuttoned my jeans, stopped, pulled her down on top of me and watched with my hands behind my head as she rode me.

"Fuck me harder Monie?" She stopped, turned around, mounted herself, grabbed the back of the loveseat and had my ass moaning like a bitch.

"I'm sorry baby. It won't happen again. Come home." She stuck her tongue in my mouth and continued riding me. I flipped her over and literally fucked the shit outta her. By the time we were finished it was after one thirty.

BANG! BANG! BANG! BANG! We heard someone about to knock the glass down.

"Hurry up and get dressed." I told Monie who appeared to be as confused as me. The person banged on it again.

"Stand over there." I had her move behind me in case some shit kicked off. She was already on the phone calling her brother.

"WHAT?" I shouted when the sliding door and curtains opened.

"Aww shit." Haven said. I noticed the same bitch Monie beat up standing next to him.

"Aww shit what?"

"You made me crawl outta my girl pussy to come here for my cousins' husband?" Haven stared at the woman.

"Haven he almost broke my wrist and the chick he was with dragged me down the steps. This is supposed to be a safe working environment." The chick said.

"What's the problem?" Monie walked around me.

"Evidently, your husband almost broke her wrist and you drug her down the steps. Why didn't you tell me y'all would be here?" He asked Monie.

"It was spur of the moment and the shit with her, happened two hours ago. Why is she just now telling you?" Monie questioned with her arms folded.

"Mannnn, I don't fucking know." Haven looked aggravated at the woman.

"Look, she approached me at the bar asking if I'm from outta town, then followed me to get a VIP area. She took it upon herself to strip and try to feel my dick. You damn right I was about to break her wrist. I told you I was married and not interested. You tried me and got what you got." I said and turned to grab my things to go.

"Now Tamara, you may not know he's my husband but as an employee, you know better than to be persistent to a customer if he tells you no. Am I right Haven?"

"Did he tell you he was married and not interested?" I waited for this bitch to lie.

"He didn't..." I went to open my mouth and Haven stopped me.

"I know for a fact he's not gonna lie about being married because this nigga strung out on his wife." I sucked my teeth and Monie looked at me.

"Anyway, you're fired and if you got an issue with what took place here, I'm sure I can find the video with you stalking him."

"Haven, you know I need this job." She whined.

160

"Not my problem. Beat it." He walked off with her running behind.

"Why didn't he press the red button to open the door?" I asked because its there.

"He always knocks a few times first and then he'll press it." She grabbed her things and stood in front of me.

"You're not strung?" Monie questioned and stared at me.

"Maybe I should..." I pushed her gently to the balcony.

"You should what? I dare you to say it." I was in front of her with my hands under her shirt.

"VJ, we're out in the open."

"So. You're my wife and no one can see anything." She moaned a little in my ear.

"You know I love when you..." I stopped her from speaking.

"Hold on." I moved her away from the balcony and zoned in on the dance floor.

"What's wrong?"

"That bitch is here." I went towards the stairs and turned back around to grab Monie. I couldn't take a chance of anyone bothering her.

"Baby what's going on?"

"Hurry up. It's Latifa." We both moved through the crowd. When we made it to the spot Latifa was at, she was gone.

"Let's go." I gripped her hand tighter and had her following me out the door.

"I don't want you going anywhere alone again. Do you hear me?" I walked to my car and hit the alarm. I waited for her to get in and searched the parking lot. No Latifa in sight but I'm gonna find her and put her six feet deep with Freddy.

"We'll pick your truck up in the morning." She nodded and put her seatbelt on.

"Yo! How you know I was here anyway?" I asked and pulled off.

"The chick who took your card told me. She said your husband is here and thirsty ass Tamara tryna hit on him."

"You know Tamara?" I questioned because if she knew her, why was the bitch hitting on me?

"Not really. I know she's been working here for a minute and hear stories about her."

"How the other chick know I'm your husband?"

"We're on Ariel's Instagram page." She showed me the pictures Ariel had on her page.

"Oh. What if I didn't want her to call you?"

"VJ, I'm not about to play this game with you. How did you say it? If you ever mess up, we'll be on some murder suicide shit." I busted out laughing.

I loved my ride or die wife but she's gonna hate me tomorrow because I'm about to really show her who's boss in the bedroom.

Haven

"Everything ok?" Ariel asked waiting for me in the bed. We had just finished having sex when the manager called me in about Tamara. She explained how the girl at the front told her, some guy was drunk, went to VIP, Tamara followed him and all hell broke loose. I told them to handle it because my ass was tired.

Unfortunately, she called me back because Tamara wanted to press charges and all this other bullshit. However; when I get there, I find out it's VJ. I knew then, Monie was lurking and it must've been her who whooped Tamara's ass.

I meant what I said about VJ being strung out on my cousin. He has to be in order to be her first, get her pregnant, marry her and then kill two people for her thus far. Ain't no man doing that for just anybody.

Being strung doesn't necessarily mean it's about the sex. Even though it's been some shit every time we're around one another, you can tell in his actions and words how in love with Monie he is. He caters to her, fought me over her and the fact he didn't want her to see death is another factor. Yea, I let Ariel see me torture my ex sister in law but when she asked to watch me kill her, I shut it down the same as VJ. Some have the stomach for it and others don't. Plus, Ariel sees enough at her job and I'm not about to be the cause of nightmares

"I fired Tamara."

"Why?" She rolled over and laid on my chest. I explained what happened and she agreed Tamara had to go.

"What were they doing at the club? Well Monie because I thought they weren't speaking."

"I had to bang on the VIP door in order for them to open it so I'm sure you know what they were doing." I don't even wanna think about any of the women in my family having sex and here the damn door was closed and so were the curtains.

"Good."

"Good?" I questioned.

"She thought he'd leave her." I started laughing.

"If his ass hasn't left her after all he's been through to be with her, he ain't going nowhere."

"Oh, like I was gonna leave you."

"Yea right." She waved me off because we both know she's not going nowhere.

"Would you say yes if I asked you to marry me?" She lifted her head and looked at me.

"If that's a proposal..."

"Man relax. I just asked a question. Ain't nobody proposing." She punched me in the chest.

"You didn't answer the question." I put my hand behind my head and stared. I'd never thought she and I would link up. All we did is argue and bump heads. Now look. She's about to have my babies and be my wife.

"You'd have to ask." I mushed her in the head.

"Haven, I don't want to answer yes and you say oh, I wasn't gonna ask because you have a smart ass mouth." She laid back down and moved closer to me.

"Yo. If you move any closer, I'm gonna fall off the bed." I heard her suck her teeth. I laughed and thought about the ring I'm gonna have to buy.

****

"Haven!" I turned to see Sharika standing with her son outside the mall. I blew my breath in the air because I already know she's about to get on my nerves.

"Sit over there Ant." She pointed to the bench by the door.

"Are you really not gonna help me anymore?"

"Did you graduate high school?" I asked.

"Yes why?"

"Because I'm tryna figure out why you don't understand the word no." I stared down at her.

"I've seen them together. Do you know he brought her a truck? The bitch is rolling in diamonds and I saw her at the salon on Broad street." I stopped her because that's my aunt Venus shop.

"First off, you're a got damn stalker." She sucked her teeth.

"Second, how do you know what he brought her? Wait! Let me guess. Instagram." She gave me a fake smile.

"Why is she posting those things? It's like she's taunting me."

"How the fuck she taunting you and has no idea who you are?" She couldn't answer.

"Did you approach her at the shop?"

"No. The owner would probably beat my ass."

"She would." It was my turn to give the phony smile. My aunt Venus don't play that petty shit.

"You need to get a life and let the boy meet his father." I tried to walk past and she stopped me.

"For what? Her to try and be me? No thanks."

"Sharika let me ask you this." She was about to walk away and stopped.

"Are you really mad at the woman, or mad the woman is getting everything you wanted?" She smirked.

"I'm mad the bitch is tryna be me."

"What the hell is wrong with you?" I grabbed her by the arm and moved to the corner.

"The woman don't know you and you're assuming she wants your life. Look, I don't know what type of crazy meds you're on, but you need to up the dosage because you out here bugging."

"Take your hands off my mom." Her son yelled and came running over.

"Boy you know not to try me." He stopped short.

"Exactly. Take your mom home and make sure she takes the medicine her doctor gave her."

"Haven don't tell him that."

"My bad. Tell your mom to go to the doctors because she needs crazy people meds." I mushed him and turned to her.

"Haven why you mush that kid?" I turned and saw Monie walking up with VJ and Legend was in the stroller. He stood off to the side while she and I spoke.

"Man, this bitch crazy."

"Hi. I'm his cousin Monie." She reached her hand out to shake and Sharika gave her a look.

"Do we know each other?" Monie asked and pulled away.

"Is there a problem with my wife?" Now VJ came towards her. She damn near shit on herself and tried to hide her son.

"The hell wrong with you?" I asked.

"No problem."

"What's wrong ma?" The little boy asked.

"Yo, who's his father?" VJ asked staring.

"No one from around here."

"Bitch his dad is from around here. You just said..." I barked.

"Bye Haven." She rushed off with her son and kept looking back.

"Is that your baby?" Monie asked and both of us waited for him to answer.

"Hell no. I don't know that chick, but her son looks familiar as fuck. Like I've seen him before."

"Ariel said the same thing." We looked at Sharika rushing to her car.

"Did she say who is dad is?" He asked and Monie looked at both of us.

"Nah she don't know either. She said it'll come to her one day. A'ight I'm out." I walked off to go into Tiffany's.

I made an appointment to look at rings and Sharika had me five minutes late as it was. I'm definitely gonna ask my girl if she remembers who the boy's dad is because you would've thought her ass seen a ghost when VJ walked up.

"Hi. Mr. Banks." The man shook my hand and took me in the back.

"Ok, so you mentioned the type of ring you wanted, and this is what we've come up with. These are as close as we can get." He pulled out two cases of rings and all of them had high ass price tags. I guess Ariel is worth it. I mean she did purchase her own house and now has me living with her. She doesn't have a mortgage, fucks me real good, about to have my kid and run an entire hospital. I'd say she's worth these prices.

"This one." I lifted a big ass heart shaped ring similar to the one Cardi B has but it's a light shade of blue.

"This ring costs..."

"I don't care how much it cost. Put it in that Velcro box thing and wrap it up." He nodded with a smile and twenty minutes later I was walking out with a damn engagement ring. I need a drink.

171

Colby Jr.

"Shit Ciara. Your pussy feels good and different." I had my side chicks' legs on my shoulder as I continued giving her the business. Yup, this is the same one who informed me about my girl cheating.

"I'm pregnant Colby." She moaned out and I should stop but I couldn't. It's a possibility the baby is mine.

After she mentioned Jacinta cheating and showed me proof, I ended up staying the night with her. I was hurt like a motherfucker hearing my girl dipped out but even more hurt, it was with someone close or should I say, I brought on and became close with.

Ciara an I fucked off and on for days with no protection. A few times I didn't pull out and now here we are.

Ciara was an ok looking chick. Nothing too fancy about her but she was loyal and never once, stepped outta line when Jacinta was around. No one knew about our affair except family and that's because I brought her over a few times. My mom had a fit because she was cool with my girl but my father and uncles didn't care one way or another. It's funny because Ariel and Armonie liked Ciara more and told me to leave Jacinta hundreds of times.

Jacinta loved me at one point, I guess. She was Spanish with a great body and I was her first sexual partner. I taught her a lot and to know another man received the same pleasure didn't sit right with me. I know what VJ meant when he said, another man will never envision what it's like to have his wife in bed. He'll be the only one to ever know.

I never expected Jacinta to step out and had she not, I probably would've married her. Not sure I would've stopped cheating, but she'd have my last name.

"Make me cum Colby." I put Ciara's legs down, pressed my lips against hers and gave her what she asked for. I had no business releasing inside her. She did mention being pregnant, so it really didn't matter at this point.

"How far are you?" I rested my body next to hers.

"Four weeks." I knew then it's definitely a possibility the child could be mine. We've been fucking without protection for about that long or longer.

173

"A'ight." I rolled over and picked my phone up to find an abortion clinic.

"My appointment is tomorrow." I turned to look at her. I didn't know she made an appointment already.

"I'm not ready for kids Colby and neither are you." I didn't disagree.

"Then why aren't you on birth control?"

"I'm gonna start the pill after tomorrow." She sat up.

"I know it's asking a lot but can you take me?"

"What time?"

"First thing in the morning. I have to be there by seven to sign in and do the paperwork. The actual abortion is scheduled for 8:15."

"You ok?" I asked because we may not be ready for kids but we knew the consequences. I didn't want children yet but she looked sad discussing it.

"I'm ok. Just scared. I've heard stories and..."

"And I'll be right there." We kissed again and before I knew it, we were back at it.

The next day, she woke me up at six and both of us started to get ready. She wasn't allowed to eat or drink but my ass was starving. I picked something up on the way but wasn't gonna eat it until she went to get the procedure. It'll be cold but who cares?

We stepped in and it was one other couple there who looked too damn old to be here. He had to be in his 60's and she was maybe 30.

Ciara went to the desk, grabbed the clipboard and filled out the paperwork. I told the lady I'm paying and handled the financial part before she went to the back. A half hour later, Ciara kissed me and was gone.

"What?" I answered the phone for Jacinta as I waited for Ciara to finish.

"Where are you?"

"None of your got damn business." I took a bite of my sandwich and glanced back at the TV.

"Colby, what's wrong? You've been acting funny lately." The bitch had the nerve to ask. I hadn't mentioned knowing about Will but she should've known I'd find out.

"I'll be there shortly. Don't leave." I hung up and continued waiting.

Before I went home, I made sure Ciara was comfortable and left her money for food and anything else she needed. The doctor said she had to be on bed rest for at least a week. I told him I'd be the one checking on her, so she'll follow directions.

On the way out, I saw an envelope with a doctor's office name on it. I opened it up and it was the test results from her pregnancy and all the STD's she's been tested for. Everything came back normal, which I'm happy about because it's no telling who else my girl slept with and loyal or not, Ciara could've dipped out. She don't owe me shit.

I put the paper back in the envelope and went to my house to deal with the next issue.

"Jacinta where you at?" She must not have heard me because when I went upstairs, she stood in the bathroom crying.

"What?"

"I'm pregnant." It's like the wind was knocked right outta me. How do I go from getting rid of one kid to possibly having another?

"Whose is it?"

"Excuse me?" I wanted to wring her neck so bad.

"Is it mine or Will's?" She stood there quiet. I started the shower hopped in and went about my business. When I returned, she was knocked out. I laid on the opposite side of our California king bed and fell asleep.

"Ssss. Oh damn." I grabbed Jacinta's hips and slammed her down harder on my dick.

"I love you Colby and I'm sorry for everything." It was at this moment, she admitted in her own way, she cheated. After I brought it up that day, she never said a word.

I sat up, flipped her over and took all my frustrations out on her. After we finished, I showered and left the house. Call me fucked up but Ciara needed me the most right now. She was able to wash and everything, but I wanted to help her. It's crazy because I never once considered making her my main and she knew it.

****

"GET THE FUCK UP!" I shouted after coming in the house.

"Colby I'm tired."

"Tired of what? Burning motherfuckers?" I felt a sensation in my dick yesterday but assumed it to be a bladder infection or something.

I went to the doctors and he gave me a medication to help. Today, he calls and tells me I have gonorrhea and need to come in for a shot. I know he had to be bugging because I saw the results from Ciara. So I know the only person who could've given it to me is Jacinta.

I didn't plan on sleeping with Jacinta but the last few days, she's woke me up with either head or sex.

"You going to the doctors." I didn't mention anything else.

"Why you yelling?" She got out the bed, handled her business and I drove her to the damn emergency room because they give you results right away. Doctors' offices make you wait 24 hours or longer.

178

"Ms. Martinez you have gonorrhea and you're two months pregnant." The doctor said in a concerned voice.

"I fucking knew it." I paced the hospital floor mad as hell.

"All the other blood test will be back in a few days and we'll call you if we need to send you other medication. Meanwhile, we have to give you a shot to get rid of the STD." The doctor told her and left the room to get the stuff. She had the nerve to cry.

"Is he the only one you fucked?" I asked.

"How we know you didn't give it to me?" I chuckled.

"I'm about to hurt your feelings real quick and when I'm done, don't say shit to me and find your way home." I closed the door.

"What?"

"First of all, the one chick I did fuck without a condom, don't have shit because I saw her paperwork; recent too. Second, I allowed her to get rid of my kid because I couldn't hurt you like that even after knowing you fucked my boy." Her eyes were damn near blinding her from the amount of tears falling.

"And third, we will never be together again and if that's my kid, we'll co-parent."

"Colby please don't do this."

"I have never brought you back a disease Jacinta. NEVER!" I shouted making her jump. I'd never put my hands on her.

"I fucked up and I'll never say I was the perfect boyfriend but one thing you can say is, no woman has ever told you if we messed around. No woman could ever tell you I said, I loved her and no woman will ever say, I mentioned leaving you because through all my shit, you remained the wife."

"It doesn't make it right."

"Then you should've left me instead of staying around to keep the Banks title." She stared at me.

"I know you loved the power my family's name brought. You loved living in the lap of luxury and shitting on bitches with your expensive clothes, shoes, purses, vacations, cars and the house but guess what?" I walked over to her.

"All you did is prove you were only with me for the money. A real woman would've left me for good or made me fight to have her in my life. All you were worried about is materialistic shit and tryna hurt me."

"I loved you Colby." She cried out when I opened the door.

"You're right. You loved me and now you don't." I left her sitting on the stretcher and walked out. I called up my cousin Haven, met him at the hotel and took the elevator to the basement.

"I'm sorry bro. She pursued me." Will shouted as I put my black gloves on.

"She has a different story."

"Colby come on. You know my family and..."

"And you knew my girl. You never bite the hand that feeds you." I took the chainsaw outta Jax's hand and went to work. I loved cutting people up. Something about hearing the bones crack and the screams made my adrenaline pump.

"You good?" Haven asked after I finished.

"Never been better. Let's go for a drink." He nodded to the cleanup crew and me and my Banks family bounced to Haven's club. What a damn day.

VJ

"Happy Birthday baby." Monie led me outside in a blindfold to get my gift.

"The freaky ass birthday sex was enough Monie."

"Nope. I got you this too." She told me to hold Legend while she took the blindfold off.

"NO SHIT!" I shouted when I stared at the navy blue and black 2019 BMW i8. It was top of the line and this specific model only had three other ones in the whole world.

"It's yours." I handed Legend back to her and ran over to the car like a kid. She said she had to record it for Brayden because he said I'd act like a kid when I saw it. He wasn't lying. This shit is fire.

"Da Da." Both of us looked at Legend when he said his first words. He just turned six months and Monie tried like hell to get him to say ma ma first.

"That's right man. Come here." He reached out for me and I sat him on my lap. Monie went on the passenger side and I wouldn't unlock the door.

"Tell mommy this is our chick magnet car."

"Tell daddy, mommy will fuck him up if a bitch even gets close to this car." I busted out laughing and unlocked it.

"You good?" I asked when she sat. She's four months pregnant and I'm worried about her dilating early again.

"I'm fine babe. This car is too damn low." I leaned over and kissed her.

"Thank you Monie."

"I have another surprise for you later."

"I don't want anymore." Me and Legend were looking in the car. He was playing with the steering wheel, while I looked at the gadgets.

"Too bad. Come on because your mom wants you over for a birthday lunch."

"She knows I'm grown right?"

"You're her first born VJ. Give her a break." I laughed.

"I love you more than I can ever say or show you Armonie Davis."

"And I love you the same Vernon Davis Junior and don't you ever forget it." We kissed again and this time much

184

longer. Had Legend not blew the horn we would've still been out there.

"Legend you can't be drawing attention. The ladies will come to you." I lifted him in the air a few times. My son was hysterical laughing.

I stepped in the shower and as bad as I wanted her to join me, she had to get Legend ready. Once I finished, I took over and watched him until she was done.

We drove to my parents' house and stayed there all day. My siblings stopped by and so did my aunts, uncles and cousins who came to town for my surprise.

****

"Where we going Monie?" I asked because she had me wear this blue Tom Ford suit, which means the place must be expensive. She wore a dark blue strapless dress to match, with a pair of Jimmy Choo heels. We both rocked our diamonds and stepped out.

"This drives nice babe." We were in my car and of course I had to test out the speed limit. She hated it already because she was pregnant and felt huge tryna get in and out.

"What's this?" I pointed to the building that looked deserted from the outside.

"Just come on." She said and I parked in the front and helped her out. She unlocked the door with the key and stepped in.

"It's dark as fuck in here. Where the lights at?" I said and tried to find the switch.

"Right here." I shut them on.

"SURPRISE!" Everyone shouted and he turned to me.

"You did all this?" I pointed to the decorations, water statues, the cages on pedestals, food, the DJ, the made up dance floor and a stage.

"I did." I placed my hands on her face and kissed her deep and passionate. I appreciated the fuck outta my wife for doing all this.

"My pussy wet VJ." I started laughing and took her hand in mine. Everyone started saying happy birthday and some even handed me cards. After a half hour, the DJ had everyone sit to eat and shortly after, the real party started.

"Oh shit." I shouted. The cages lit up and half naked women appeared in each one.

"You like so far?"

"I do but why aren't you stripping for me?"

"Don't you worry. I got something special for you." She pecked my lips and left me sitting with Brayden and the other guys.

"Can we get the birthday guy to the center of the floor?" I stood and walked over to the chair some chick put out. The crowd dispersed to the sides and I saw men helping the women out the cages. What the hell did Armonie set up?

"Ok Mr. Davis. Your wife said to enjoy this but no touching." The DJ spoke on the mic and everyone started laughing with me. I sat in the chair with my arm hanging on the back.

Please me baby, turn around and just tease me baby, you know what I want and what I need baby...

The new song by Cardi B and Bruno Mars played in the background as the women from the cages and a few more came out and started dancing in front of me. All the men crowded around to watch but who I wanted to see hadn't shown her face yet. Yea these women were beautiful and had banging bodies, but no one could top my wife.

The music played a little longer and then cut off. The women made a wall with their bodies and the lights went out as the next song played. The women slowly moved out the way as the intro started.

What y'all know about a, supermodel, fresh outta Elle magazine, buy her own bottles, look pimp juice I need me one, bad than a mutha. I need a bad girl.

Ushers song *Bad Girl* played and out walked my wife in an all-black cat suit and some heels. I'm making her leave them on when we get home.

The zipper was down in the front and even with her stomach poking out she was the baddest one in here. She turned around, dropped it low and once she started twerking, I had to grab my dick to calm it down. She knew my ass was ready to fuck because she smirked looking over her shoulder.

By the time the song was over, she was on my lap facing me. My hands were all over her. I've never in my life had a woman strip for me the way she did. Yea I've seen strippers and of course they want the money but for my wife to put on a show for me, had me at a loss for words.

"Happy Birthday."

"It sure is." Her arms draped my neck as we began kissing like no one else was in the room.

"I love you baby." She whispered in my ear and rested her head on my shoulder.

"Ok bitchhh. You did your thing for him." Ariel tapped her on the shoulder.

"What's wrong?" I noticed how slow she moved to lift her head.

"Nothing. The dance tired me out. Can you get me a water?" She asked Ariel and I stood with her still attached and went to the table.

"You wanna go home?" I asked.

"No baby. I'm ok." She smiled and drank the water Ariel brought over.

"Bitch, I'm fucking copying. I don't care. When you see me do it for Antoine, don't talk shit." Vanity said to Monie.

"As long as you use different songs." Monie joked and rested her head against the seat.

"I told him it was ok. Please don't be mad." My wife grabbed my hand and asked me to sit next to her.

"Mad about what?"

"I invited him to your party. I'm sorry." She started tearing up like the cry baby she is when she's pregnant.

"Come here Ariel." We all turned around when Haven got on the microphone. Armonie squeezed my hand.

"Monie, I am aggravated about that because you know we don't fuck with each other but if he about to do what I think he is, then I guess it's ok."

"I love you so much baby and I promise not to do anything without telling you again."

"You gonna strip for me at home?" I let my finger dip in her cleavage.

"Whatever you want baby." She sat on my lap as we watched Ariel walk over to Haven.

Haven

"Come here Ariel." I spoke into the microphone on the stage. She turned around and I smiled at how big her stomach was. Seeing her with my child inside only made what I'm about to do worth it.

"Haven what are you doing up there?" She asked still walking towards me. The room seemed very quiet and all eyes were on me. At the moment, I was at a loss for words, but she knew what it was because those tears falling down her face as I got down on one knee, were all I needed to see.

"Oh shit." I heard Brayden say and people started crowding around.

"I don't know what to say so I'm just gonna give you this ring and you can make up any speech you want in your head." I opened the box, and everyone gasped.

"Once you got down on your knee, I didn't need a speech. I know who you are baby, and I accept this as your proposal. I love you so much and yes I'll marry you." She took a seat on the stage and I slid the ring on her finger. Everyone clapped and Ariel leaned in for a kiss. I looked up and VJ nodded in my direction. Maybe it's his way of congratulating me.

When I mentioned proposing to Ariel at my grams house, Monie told me to do it here because all the family would be in attendance. I didn't want to but she whined like a baby and grams said it's a good idea. Of course, I had an issue because me and dude don't speak and it's his party. I'm not sure I'd be ok with it. I saw his facial expression when I called Ariel on stage, but I know he won't cause a scene either.

"You say enough at home Haven. I know this pussy got you stuck." She whispered in my ear making me laugh.

"Very stuck." I honestly told her.

Ariel and I were frenemies first and knew a lot about one another. Our families were cool and even though Juicy is the one I assumed I'd marry; Ariel is the one who locked me down. She had my heart even after I said love didn't live here anymore.

"Congratulations. Yayyy. I'm so happy for you." Monie said after people came over to congratulate us.

"You ok?" I asked because she liked fatigue.

"I'm fine. The dance took a lot outta me."

"I'll be back. You going to sit with your mom right?" VJ asked.

"Yea." He kissed her cheek and walked out the side door.

"Sit." I traded spots with her and went to smoke myself.

"Haven no shit."

"Bye Ariel." I saw Colby Jr and Jax coming towards me.

"Everybody getting married out this bitch." VJ said to Brayden who proposed to his chick last night. They've been through hell and high water too.

"Antoine you next?" VJ told him

"Ring already being made. Ain't no other man touching her. That's me all day." He was proud of his woman. Vanity was definitely a beautiful woman and he'd be a fool not to lock her down.

"Don't forget our meeting Haven." Marco Jr said patting me on the shoulder. He wants me to do some reaper shit for him.

"You got it." All of us stood out there smoking and shit was cool until Ariel stepped out bugging.

"Haven why this bitch on my Instagram saying y'all fucked?"

"Huh?"

"Ugh oh." Colby Jr. joked.

"I posted my ring and she said..." I snatched the phone out her hand and noticed it was Marlena. I walked away holding Ariel hand and called the bitch on my phone.

"I knew she'd tell you and I'd hear from you." Is what Marlena said when she answered.

"Why you lying to my fiancé?"

"I miss you Haven." I didn't even have the energy to argue right now with her.

"Bet. I'll be by to see you later. I'ma take you to a hotel."

"Are you speaking in front of your girl?" She asked and Ariel smiled. She knew what the hotel was about.

"Nah, she walked away. I'll call when I'm on my way." I hung up.

"I love you Haven." Ariel kissed me and went back in. This chick had my head gone. Oh well, she's what I need to calm down.

I finished smoking, stayed a little longer and went to handle Marlena. Oh she was ecstatic to see me, but she wasn't so happy when we made it to the basement.

****

"Yo! Where your husband at?" I asked Monie when she opened the door.

"In the back. What's wrong?" She closed the door behind me.

"Nothing. Where's the back?" I had no clue where anything was because it's my first time here. When he moved her in with him, I never got an invite.

"I know you better not be here to fight because..."

196

"Monie I'd never do that again in front of you. I apologized already. You want me to say it again?"

"Monie, what's taking so long?" VJ walked in wearing basketball shorts and T-shirt. Their son was on his shoulders.

"Haven stopped by to see you."

"Where you wanna meet because we not fighting in front of my family again?" I chuckled; yet, understood why he felt that way.

"Take Legend upstairs Monie." He removed him off his shoulders.

"What's going on?" Vanity, Ariel and grams came inside.

"Ariel what you doing here? You supposed to be at the store."

"Hey babe. I stopped by after work to show my wedding dress to Monie. Vanity and grams were here already. What you doing here?" She stood in front of me and folded her arms.

"Let me put some clothes on." VJ said.

197

"Nah. I'm not here for that." He stopped and stared along with all of them.

"I just stopped through to say Latifa, her mother, father and aunt are no longer here."

"Where you'd find her?" VJ asked.

"She brought her dirty ass in the club last night and I had Jerome follow her. Evidently, she's been staying a few towns over; which is why no one could find her. The mom was still with the sister, but the dad stayed with her. In any case, they're gone, and I had Brayden send the photos to your phone." He felt his waist and realized it wasn't on him.

"Did you torture her?" Monie asked and I laughed.

"No. Jax did."

"Jax?"

"Yea. Him and Valley seemed to be close now so he asked if they could do it."

"My brother Valley?" VJ asked and handed Monie the phone. Her, Vanity, grams and Ariel looked at the photos. He only sent the ones of them tied up in the torture room. They didn't need to see the aftermath.

"Let me talk to you real quick." I went to the front door and stepped on the porch.

"Monie is my favorite cousin and even though no man is good enough for the women in my family, she's special and I think you know why." He folded his arms.

"Actually, I don't."

"She's always been self-conscious about her legs; which is why she didn't date until that fuck nigga. She doesn't know we found out he used to tease her about it, but we did. We weren't sure if you'd do the same once you found out." He turned his face up and I shrugged my shoulders.

"Exactly. Ariel finally told me the story of what happened at the party and how Latifa shouted it out. The longer you stayed with her, the way you had her back even with me only proved you were the best man for her. Most men would've left her alone by now." I lit my blunt.

"Freddy stayed." He said and I looked at him.

"After the first few months, he stopped coming around. We didn't know she broke up with him due to cheating but when she took him back, he still stayed away from us."

"None of y'all knew he was beating her?" He questioned.

"You see how we are about her. She knew we'd kill him if we found out, which is why Monie stayed away during those times."

"Oh."

"Look." I passed him the blunt and shockingly he took it.

"We may not ever be cool and that's fine. I'll sleep fine knowing she has you protecting her and the kids."

"Always and I don't hold grudges, nor do I wanna be at functions and you popping shit. I'm not that nigga." He voiced his concern.

"I respect it." The door opened.

"How the fuck y'all out here smoking without me?" Grams snatched the blunt from VJ.

"Really?" He said and looked at her.

"Hell yea really. Now Haven, I hope you over the bullshit because you owe me all those weeks of no weed." I started laughing. She took a pull.

"VJ, I'm gonna need you to keep your dick outta my great grandbaby after this one. Her pussy needs a break." He busted out laughing.

"Sorry grams, but she got a nigga hooked. It's no way in hell I'm staying outta that." I looked at him.

"I knew your ass was strung." I said.

"If Ariel got the reaper to propose, I'd say you're the same." I nodded and the three of us stood outside smoking and talking.

"I've been meaning to ask. How did you find Mecca?" I laughed.

"Regardless of us not speaking, my cousin gave me the address Raheem stayed at. I waited for them to leave the house and followed."

"But how did you know what she looked like?" He asked.

"I admit when they left the house, I had no clue if it were her; that is until her friend told me."

"Her friend?" Grams asked.

"Yea."

"What kind of friend snitches?" She questioned and smoked some more.

"A bitch who almost had her hand broke for tryna feel me up on the dance floor." VJ shook his head.

"When I asked where Mecca was, she told me the exact outfit she wore." I told them. Lily had no problem giving her up and actually told me to kill her. She wanted Raheem as far away as possible from her.

"Was her name Lily?"

"Yup." He shook his head.

"Where's Lily?" Grams asked and opened the door to go back in.

"Same place as Mecca." I shrugged and he thanked me for finding Mecca and allowing him to take her life.

We went in and he ordered food for everyone and somehow, Brayden his girl, Colby Jr brought Ciara over and everyone else showed up. We didn't get home until four the next morning.

"Thanks babe." Ariel said when we got out the shower.

"For?"

"For putting your pride to the side and breaking bread with my cousin."

"I don't feel like hearing your mouth."

"Whatever but since you did, I think you deserve something special." She dropped her towel, had me lay on the bed, grabbed some ice and definitely had me down for the count.

Antoine

"Are you sure about marrying my daughter? I mean it's only been about two years and..."

"Vernon stop it. You were ready to marry me soon as I threw it on you. Talking about have my baby." I was cracking up listening to Vanity's parents go back and forth. They joked around all the time and I think it's why their daughter is the same.

"Man, you the one who..." Mrs. Davis stood in front of him.

"I'm the one who what? Told you we weren't getting married because you kept that ex ho of yours around?" He waved her off.

"Exactly! Stop messing with Antoine and give him your blessing." She wrapped her arms around his waist.

"He's good to her and she loves him." Her dad looked at me.

"Did she ever mention what she's been through?" He asked in a serious tone.

"As far as…?"

"Rape? Or should I say attempted because it didn't happen?"

"Hell no. When did this happen?" I had no idea what he was talking about. Vanity never mentioned it to me.

"Calm down Killa." Her father said making me feel a little better. I would've been pissed knowing someone did that to her while we were together. It's still fucked up, regardless when it happened.

"She was a freshman in high school and wanted to be like her friends and walk home." Her mom started telling me the story.

"She was literally four blocks away from our house when these guys approached her."

"How many?" I don't know why I'm asking if it happened years ago. They lived in Virginia all this time so it's not like I'd know who they were.

"Two. Anyway, her friend had just went inside and Vanity kept going. The guys followed her maybe two blocks and snatched her up. At first, they asked who she was and if they could have her number."

"Both of them?" That's weird for two guys to ask when they're together.

"From what she says, yes." Her father said with his face turned up.

"When she told them they couldn't have it, one guy held her hands as the other one started taking her pants down. Vanity started screaming but one of the guys punched her in the face; knocking her out for a few minutes." The more she told, the angrier I became.

"Right before one of then penetrated her, an old man came by yelling someone was being raped and scared them off. By then, she was fully naked. He called the cops, and the ambulance drove her to the hospital. Evidently, Vanity must've woken up and tried fighting them off because she had DNA under her nails." Her father said and stopped but her mom kept going.

"She was beaten really bad and they couldn't identify her at first. It wasn't until we weren't able to reach her that we called the cops. They informed us a teenager was brought in and it could be her." I saw her mom wiping her eyes.

"We get there and my daughters face is so swollen, you could barely tell it was her. Had it not been for the necklace her dad gave her, we probably wouldn't have known right away."

"Damn."

"Yea. It was bad." Her mom walked closer to me.

"We love all our kids the same Antoine, but we tend to cater more to Vanity because of what she's been through. Her panic attacks aren't as bad anymore and she's doing very well for herself. If you're going to marry her, we need to know you're gonna keep her safe. She has all of us and we're very close, but we also know she's grown. We can't stop her life because we're scared to let go."

"I'm gonna keep her safe and I promise not to hurt her. I think she'll kill me if I did." They both laughed which eased the tension.

"I'm serious."

"Just don't hurt her and you have our blessing." Her mother said.

"Hold up Maylan. He's supposed to smoke a blunt with me or something before we say yes."

"Vernon, VJ just dropped Legend off an hour ago and you smoked with him."

"Maylan sometimes it's ok not to talk." He told her and she picked Legend up from his high chair.

"Anyway. Do you have the ring?"

"Yea. I'm gonna propose tomorrow at my party."

"Congratulations and I have no doubt in my mind that she'll say yes." Her mom gave me a hug and Legend reached for my necklace. Vanity had him a lot too and we wanted kids. We just decided to wait until we're married.

"Thanks for y'all blessing. Gotta go Lil man. I'll see you at aunties house." I kissed his cheek. Now let me prepare my speech.

****

"I think your girl is gonna do what her brother's wife did at his party." Marco Jr said at the club. He threw me this big ass birthday bash and it was packed.

"Why you say that?"

"Look at all these bitches dressed alike." He pointed to women dressed in all black. Vanity asked if I liked what Armonie did and I told her yes but didn't see much.

As a man we definitely appreciated seeing the women before her but once Armonie stepped out, all of us went to the back to smoke. What we look like watching his woman dance for him?

"Well if she does, these niggas gotta go." Marco laughed.

"Where's Harlow?" I asked about his girlfriend.

"No clue." He searched the club for her. I actually liked her for him and so did everyone else. She's the exact opposite of what he's used to and she doesn't let him walk all over her.

"Ok y'all. We in for a treat." Armonie said on the microphone. Her stomach was starting to show so whatever's going on, I knew she wasn't partaking in it.

I looked for VJ and he was standing directly next to her. They still have yet to find Latifa so I know he's not too far. Marco and I put some shit in motion to find her though.

"Antoine you come to the front and Marco, Brayden, Colby Jr., Jax and Valley make sure you're close." She smirked and they looked at me.

"Security make sure the doors are locked. We don't need any commotion." We turned and saw them blocking the doors.

"What the hell going on?" I asked.

Look back at it, she said she never made love but she good at it, I get goosebumps when I look at it

A Boogie song played and just like Marco said, those women dressed alike formed a circle and started dancing. They had on short black jumpsuits, black hoodies and black heels. Don't ask me how they moving the way they are but I'm not mad.

The song went off and an old school one came on by Mya. I think it's called all about me. The women were doing the damn thing to the beat. The introduction to the song was long as hell.

All of a sudden out walked, Harlow, Brayden's fiancé, Colby's side chick, Jax and Valley's women and a few others. Those niggas were shocked. They started dancing and when Vanity walked out, I had to do a double take.

It's all about me tonight, I can't stop loving you, cause you're still my boo, but you gotta see, it's all about me.

I could hear the music but my girl had my full attention. She had on an all silver bodysuit with those strands or tassels hanging around the waist area. The strap up heels and glitter on her skin had my dick hard as fuck. The minute she stood in front of me, I couldn't take my eyes off. I didn't want anyone watching her but shit, I couldn't stop the show either.

Once the song ended, I lifted her up and carried her over to the stage. I could see Marco and Harlow about to fuck on the dance floor and ain't no telling where the other ones went. Shit, Armonie and VJ were damn near about to have sex next to the DJ booth.

"Can I have your attention?" The music stopped and everyone looked in our direction.

"First, let me thank my girl for the best birthday present ever." I kissed her lips and heard people clapping and a few whistles.

"Don't get fucked up in here."

"Antoine." Vanity laughed.

"Anyway, Vanity Davis you are a rare diamond, and if I had to pick you outta crowd just to make sure I could keep you in my life, I would." She smiled.

"You are more than I ever thought I deserved in a woman and I wanna know if you'll marry me?" She let my hand go as I got on one knee and covered her mouth. The ring was humongous, and I could see it shining off the lights in the club.

"Yes Antoine. Yes baby." She let me slide the ring on and kissed me with so much passion, I had to place her in front of me again because I had bricked up. I handed the DJ back the microphone and stepped down with my new fiancé.

We were congratulated for the rest of the night, but something felt off. Not with Vanity but with the vibe. I observed everyone in our area, down on the dance floor and nothing. It wasn't until I went to say something to VJ, when I noticed the person. I took off down the steps and to the door.

"Yo! What the fuck?" Marco yelled behind me.

"There's no way in hell my ex showed up here." Marco and I searched the parking lot twice and she was nowhere to be found.

"You sure you saw her?" He asked om the way back in.

"No but since I'm not, I wanted a closer look."

"I doubt she'll be back but I'll keep my eyes open too." I nodded and kept turning around to see if the person returned.

"Yo! I'm about to get Harlow ass pregnant off that dance she did for me." I started laughing.

"I'm serious. She's about to be my stripper when I get home and she don't even know it."

"Vanity already promised to do the same for me." He laughed.

"You better lock Harlow down before someone else does." I told him because if he knows like I know, she's not gonna stick around if his secrets start spilling out.

"She ain't going no fucking where." I shook my head.

"It's time you let that baggage go."

"I'm trying but it's hard." He said staring at Harlow.

"If you wanna keep her you better try harder." I told him and went to get my fiancé.

"I can't wait to get you home." Vanity whispered in my ear.

"And I can't wait to..." I was cut off when VJ and Armonie stepped in the section.

"Ok sis in law. You did that." Armonie gave both of us a hug.

"Told you I was copying. You didn't tell me how fun it was."

"Fun or not, Monie ain't doing that in front of nobody else." He and I gave each other a fist bump because neither is Vanity. Her body is for my eyes only.

Armonie

"What you think about this one?" Vanity asked regarding the wedding dress she's looking at. All of us were at this expensive bridal boutique she had to come to. After Antoine proposed, he told her to spare no expense. It's her day and nothing is too much for her.

"I don't know Vanity. It looks too old fashioned." I shrugged my shoulders. The dress had lace on the chest area and in my opinion not something I envisioned her in.

"What about this one?" Ariel wobbled over with her big ass stomach. Vanity took it and went in the dressing room.

"There's your dress." We all said at the same time. It was a fitted, strapless dress with a very long train. The sides were sheer and it so were other areas of the dress.

"What's wrong honey?" Her mom Maylan asked when she started crying.

"Do you think he can love me right?" All of us had a shocked look on our face.

"Where did they come from?"

216

"I'm scared. What if he's not done playing around with other women?"

"Has he ever cheated on you or given you a reason to believe he's unfaithful?"

"No but he's so got damn perfect in every aspect." We all started laughing.

"Antoine is at an age where he doesn't need to play around anymore. Stop looking for the bad and enjoy these moments." Her mom said.

"And get out the dress before your tears run all over it." Antoine's mom said. She took it off and all of us went out to eat.

****

"I can never get enough of being inside you." VJ moaned out as he fucked me against the wall.

"I don't ever want you to stop being inside. Baby, I'm cumming." He continued until he finished

"Remember when I said no other man will ever get the visions of making love to you?" He laid me on the bed and got in next to me.

217

"Yea."

"You make the sexiest faces I've ever seen and I'm glad I made you mine because if anyone could tell me what you look like, I'd probably kill them." I smiled and ran my hand down his face.

"It's ironic how my mom fell in love with my dad, he was her first and she's never been with anyone else. It's like de ja vu."

"If you're like your mother, I know you won't dip out."

"Never baby. VJ, you are it for me. I can't even imagine another man on top of me."

"That's all I wanna hear." He crashed his lips on mine and we went at it again. Being young and in love will have you sexing one another morning, noon and night.

Loving someone who loves you back, is a beautiful thing and I'm glad Vernon Davis Jr. is the man I'm spending the rest of my life with.

Epilogue

Ariel and Haven had their first son and he was more than happy. You couldn't tell him shit and no one was allowed to hold him unless you went by and he was out. Ariel's father opened the new research building and yup, she runs the entire place. Haven out here telling everyone she a BOSS. We never thought we'd see the day, he'd settle down and only be with one woman, but we all know it only takes one woman.

Stormy and Christian Bianca didn't get pregnant from the artificial insemination the first two times, but the third time was a charm. They had their first daughter a month ago and everyone was so happy, they threw them a party at each of their parents' house. Bianca loved the experience of being pregnant, so her and Fay are now expecting. Stormy didn't ask her sister to carry for her again but they did get a surrogate. I think after the woman spoke to Haven, Colby Jr. and the rest of the men in the family, she knew not to play games when it came to handing over the child.

VJ and Armonie are as happy as ever. VJ will still do anything for his wife; include kill again if necessary. She is the woman his parents told him were out there. Mr. Davis paid the 20k to Armonie for making him fall in love after VJ swore it would never happen. In the end, all of the families came together and now they go hard for each other; even Haven and VJ.

These books are urban fiction and I'm only here to entertain you. I know sometimes we read books and want them to end certain ways, or for the people to do what we want but it's the imagination of the writer who has the final say.

I will try my best to continue making you laugh, cry, and yell at the characters in the book. A trillion thanks for the support you all keep giving me. I am always grateful and appreciative. Love you all!!!

CPSIA information can be obtained
at www.ICGtesting.com
Printed in the USA
LVHW090325021019
632927LV00001BA/69/P